No-Hitter

The Chip Hilton Sports Series

Touchdown Pass
Championship Ball
Strike Three!
Clutch Hitter!
A Pass and a Prayer
Hoop Crazy
Pitchers' Duel
Dugout Jinx
Freshman Quarterback
Backboard Fever
Fence Busters
Ten Seconds to Play!

Fourth Down Showdown
Tournament Crisis
Hardcourt Upset
Pay-Off Pitch
No-Hitter
Triple-Threat Trouble
Backcourt Ace
Buzzer Basket
Comeback Cagers
Home Run Feud
Hungry Hurler
Fiery Fullback

For more information on
Coach Clair Bee and **Chip Hilton**
please visit us at
www.chiphilton.com

Chip Hilton Sports Series
#17

No-Hitter

Coach Clair Bee
Foreword by Jack McCallum
Updated by Randall and Cynthia Bee Farley

BROADMAN
& HOLMAN
PUBLISHERS

Nashville, Tennessee

0-8054-2096-7

Published by Broadman & Holman Publishers,
Nashville, Tennessee

Subject Heading: BASEBALL—FICTION / YOUTH
Library of Congress Card Catalog Number: 00-060846

Library of Congress Cataloging-in-Publication Data
Bee, Clair.
    No-hitter / Clair Bee ; updated by Randall and
Cynthia Bee Farley.
      p. cm. — (Chip Hilton sports series; #17)
    Summary: Chip's summer plans change when State is
selected to represent the United States in the college baseball
series with two of Japan's finest teams,and he soon finds himself
helping a Japanese college student improve his pitching.
    ISBN 0-8054-2096-7 (tp)
    [1. Baseball—Fiction. 2. Japanese—United States—Fiction.]
I. Farley, Randall K., 1952– . II. Farley, Cynthia Bee, 1952– .
III. Title.

PZ7.B381955 No   2001
[Fic]—dc21   00-060846

1 2 3 4 5 6 7 8 9 10 05 04 03 02 01

Grateful acknowledgment
is extended to

Akira Wakasugi and Susumu W. Nakamura

for their assistance to
the author in preparation of this book.

CLAIR BEE, 1959

TO

Steve and Mary Nurre and Duane and Kim Melsom

Great people and wonderful educators.
Americans in a foreign land . . .
and our longtime friends.

RANDY AND CINDY, 2001

Contents

Foreword by Jack McCallum, *Sports Illustrated*

1. . . . . . . **Asia, Here We Come!**

2. . . . . . . **Bound by Honor**

3. . . . . . . **The Friendly Skies**

4. . . . . . . **If Any of Us Can Do It**

5. . . . . . . **Down to Business**

6. . . . . . . ***Kabuki* and *Besuboru***

7. . . . . . . **Tamio-san, My Friend**

8. . . . . . . **Why Keep Score?**

9. . . . . . . **To Win His Own Game**

10. . . . . . . ***Kattobase* Hilton!**

11. . . . . . . **Face Up to a Challenge**

12. . . . . . . **The Fine Art of Baseball**

13. . . . . . . Tamio's Honorable Friends

14. . . . . . . A Third-Strike Bunt

15. . . . . . . "Boys, Be Ambitious"

16. . . . . . . "*That's* Why You Gave Him the Ball!"

17. . . . . . . The Stepping-stones

18. . . . . . . Japan's National Game

19. . . . . . . A Storybook Finish

20. . . . . . . A Moment for Diplomacy

21. . . . . . . The Rising Pitching Star

22. . . . . . . Tokyo No-Hitter

Afterword by Pat Crisp

Your Score Card

About the Author

Foreword

IT'S SOMETIMES difficult to figure out why we became who we became. Was it an influential teacher who steered you toward biology? A beloved grandparent who turned you into a machinist? A motorcycle accident that forced you into accounting?

All I know is that in my case the Chip Hilton books had something—no, a lot—to do with my becoming a sports journalist. At the very least, the books got me to sit down and read when others of my generation were watching television or otherwise goofing off; at most, they taught me many of life's lessons, about sports and sportsmanship, about coaches and coaching, about winning and losing.

Also, the books helped me, quite literally, get the job I have now. Over two decades ago, when I was a sportswriter at a small newspaper in Pennsylvania, I interviewed Clair Bee and wrote a piece about him and the Hilton books. For some strange reason, even before I met Clair, I knew I could make the story memorable, knew that meeting a legend like Clair and plumbing his mind for memories were going to be magic. They were. I sold the story to *Sports Illustrated,* and, partly because of it, I was later hired there full time.

To my surprise, and especially to the surprise of the editors at *SI,* the story produced a torrent of letters, hundreds of them, all written by closet Clair and Chip fans who, like me, had grown up on the books and never been able to forget them. Since the piece about Clair appeared in 1979, I've written hundreds of other articles, many of them cover stories about famous athletes like Michael Jordan, Magic Johnson, and Larry Bird; yet I'm still known, by and large, as the "guy who wrote the Chip Hilton story." I would safely say that still, two decades later, six months do not go by that I don't receive some kind of question about Clair and Chip.

One of the many fortunate things that happened to me as a result of that story was meeting Clair's daughter, Cindy Farley, and her husband, Randy, as well as others who could recite the starting lineups of Coach Rockwell's Valley Falls teams.

I am proud to have played a small part in the revival of Chip and the restoration of interest in Clair (not that real basketball people ever forget him). It's hard to put a finger on what exactly endures from the books, but it occurs to me that what Clair succeeded in doing was to create a universe of which we would all like to be a part.

As I leafed through one of the books recently, a memory came back to me from my days as a twelve-year-old Pop Warner football player in Mays Landing, New Jersey. A friend who shared my interest in the books had just thrown an opposing quarterback for a loss in a key game. As we walked back to the huddle, he put his arm on my shoulder pads and, conjuring up a Hilton gang character, whispered, "Another jarring tackle by Biggie Cohen." No matter how old you get, you never forget something like that. Thank you, Clair Bee.

JACK McCALLUM
Senior Writer, *Sports Illustrated*

CHAPTER 1

Asia, Here We Come!

ROBERT "SOAPY" SMITH, the redheaded, freckle-faced sophomore athlete, plopped his last suitcase on the floor and then sat on it to zip the bulging bag closed. Satisfied, he hoisted it upright and struck a dramatic pose. "Taa daa! Seoul and Tokyo," he exploded, "here we come!"

Soapy's tall, broad-shouldered roommate appeared in the doorway. His clean face and shoulders glistened with beads of water as he dried his short blond hair with a huge bath towel. "You sure make a lot of noise for one person," Chip Hilton said, grinning at his roommate. "You'll wake up the whole dorm."

"Huh!" Soapy snorted. "There hasn't been anyone around here since finals were over!"

"What about Biggie, Speed, Red, and Fireball?"

"Those guys?" Soapy asked sarcastically. "They're still at Pete's restaurant, eating him out of food and themselves out of the league." He pulled in his stomach, thrust out his shoulders, and continued self-righteously, "You don't see me being an oinker, do you?"

"How about all those shakes and banana splits?" Chip deadpanned.

"Now, Chip, you know Mr. Grayson expects me to invent new creations and combinations for the customers. When I eat all that stuff, I'm just doing my duty."

"Oh, sure!" Chip agreed.

Soapy changed the subject. "Well, that's the last suitcase," he said thankfully, wiping the perspiration from his freckled face. "We won't feel much like doing any packing at four o'clock tomorrow morning. And I've still got room in my carry-on for my toothbrush and stuff plus a change of clothes. Man, it's going to be a long flight.

"I'm just glad we already took everything else in the room home for the summer. This place looks like it did the first day we walked in as freshmen. I guess the athletic department will use this place to house their summer campers; I just hope they paint it before we get back to school." He paused and wrinkled his forehead. "There was something else . . . ."

"Looks like you couldn't have forgotten anything, judging from the size of those two suitcases and carry-on," Chip teased.

Soapy looked puzzled. "No, I mean there's something—"

"It'll come back to you," Chip comforted, glancing at his watch. "By the way, did you say good-bye to everyone?"

Soapy groaned. "That's the only bad thing about this trip."

"I know," Chip said. "I talked to or E-mailed everyone this afternoon."

"Did you see Mitzi?" Soapy asked nonchalantly, pretending to adjust the nametags on his suitcases.

Chip grinned. "Sure," he said, watching his friend closely. "She told me to make sure you don't fall in love with a beautiful Korean or Japanese girl."

Soapy's head shot up and his blue eyes sparkled. "She did? All right!" Then his face sobered. "I'm sure going to miss my parents," he said sadly. "But we might not get another chance to go play ball in Asia."

"That's what Mom said," Chip agreed. "I was counting on spending a lot of time with her this summer, but she said I shouldn't let this opportunity slip away. Besides, we'll be back in about four weeks. I'm glad we got to spend a few days at home after our last exam though."

"Imagine!" Soapy chortled gleefully, flopping onto his bed. "Chip Hilton and Soapy Smith are giving clinics in Seoul and playing baseball in Tokyo. Sure is a long way from Valley Falls, isn't it?"

Chip nodded. "It sure is. I can hardly wait 'til we leave."

Soapy examined the thumb of his right hand. "You think Rock will let me play in the first game?"

"How does it feel?"

"Great! Well, it ought to! It was hurt in the semifinal game. Let's see—" Soapy paused to add up the days. "That makes it seventeen days ago."

"It doesn't seem that long ago," Chip mused.

"Well, it is," Soapy said. "It was in the top of the eighth against Northwest at Austin."

"I thought it was in the last inning."

Soapy shook his head. "Uh-uh. That's when I threw the ball over Crowell's head, over second base." He reflected a moment and added wryly, "And nearly threw the championship away with it."

"No harm done," Chip said gently. "We won."

"Sure! Thanks to you. Do you think they have good teams over there? Teams good enough to give us some competition?"

"Of course. Lots of them. What makes you think we're unbeatable?" Chip asked.

"We won the national championship, didn't we?"

"We did do that."

"Doesn't that make us the best college team in the country?" Soapy demanded.

"Maybe. But it doesn't make us the best college team in Japan."

"We'll see about that," Soapy said. "I've got the items . . . no, itemized, no . . . itinerary! Yeah, that's it, right here." He pulled the trip itinerary out of his carry-on and scanned the dates.

STATE UNIVERSITY ATHLETIC DEPARTMENT GOODWILL ASIAN TOUR
Travel Itinerary

June 6 Wed. (Day 1)	Depart University Airport 7:10 A.M. (UAL 3382) Depart San Francisco International Airport 11:00 A.M. (UAL 807)
June 7 Thurs. (Day 2)	Arrive Kimpo International Airport (Seoul) 3:10 P.M. Transfer to Hotel (Dragon Hill) at Yongsan Dinner and Movie on the Base
June 8 Fri. (Day 3)	Baseball Clinics at Seoul International School and Seoul Foreign School State Baseball Squad Meets at Olympic Stadium Afternoon: Seoul National College of Physical Education Evening Game at Yongsan, State vs. M.A.S.H. 4077 Team
June 9 Sat. (Day 4)	Tour Demilitarized Zone (DMZ) with USO Group Tae Kwon Do Exhibition at Kukiwon (Hannam-dong) Shopping in Itaewon Team Practice Dinner Guests of Dr. Kim Myoung Hwan and Park Bong Kwon (Olympic gold medalist, tae kwon do)
June 10 Sun. (Day 5)	A.M.: Church Services P.M.: Game at Yongsan, State vs. Jets (Osan Air Base Team)
June 11 Mon. (Day 6)	Depart Kimpo International Airport (Seoul) 10:15 A.M. (UA 884) Arrive Narita International Airport (Tokyo) 12:30 P.M. Transfer to Imperial Hotel (Tokyo) Sightseeing and Dinner
June 12 Tues. (Day 7)	Practice and Sightseeing
June 13 Wed. (Day 8)	Practice and Sightseeing
June 14 Thurs. (Day 9)	Games Begin in Tokyo State vs. Waseda
Important: Consult game schedule provided by State University baseball coaches	
July 7 Sat. (Day 32)	Depart Narita International Airport (Tokyo) 4:00 P.M. (UA 852)
July 7 Sat.	Arrive San Francisco International Airport 9:20 A.M. (UA 831) Depart for individual home-connecting flights

"Let's see. This is Tuesday, the fifth of June. We leave from here tomorrow morning at seven o'clock for San Francisco. From there we catch United's international flight to Seoul, South Korea, at 11:00 A.M. on flight 807. Think we'll get upgrades for the flight? We stay in Seoul until the eleventh. Then we fly to Tokyo. We arrive in Tokyo on Monday. On Thursday we play our first game in Japan against Waseda University. So," he concluded triumphantly, "it seems logical to me that on that night, we'll be the champions of Japan."

"Why?"

"Why? Because Waseda only won the Japanese University League Championship, and it wasn't that big a deal. I read about it on the 'Net."

"But we're going to be in Japan for over three weeks."

"Meaning what?" Soapy argued stubbornly.

"Meaning we're going to play a lot of games, Soapy," Chip explained. "Beating Waseda one game won't prove anything. Besides, Keio University is just as good as Waseda."

"How do you know?"

"Frank Okada said so."

"That's it!" Soapy said excitedly. "That's what I was trying to remember." He leaped to his feet and pointed to a small box on the windowsill. "The plant! What are you going to do with Frank's tree?"

"I don't know. I forgot all about it in the rush to finish exams and then get ready for the trip," Chip worried.

In the brief silence that followed, Chip's thoughts drifted back to the beginning of his friendship with Frank Okada. Early in the season he had noticed the young Japanese student who sat in the stands day after day watching the practices. One afternoon Chip had walked over and asked if Frank wanted to "toss a few" until Coach Rockwell took the field. Frank had been delighted, and Chip found time almost every afternoon before practice to play catch with his new acquaintance.

A firm friendship had ripened between the two since that first day. And, as Chip pitched the Statesmen to victory after victory, Frank Okada became an enthusiastic baseball fan. As they came to know each other better, Chip learned that Frank was an exchange student at University High School and lived with his uncle, a State University professor in the modern languages department.

Baseball was the only relaxation Frank permitted himself. The slender, likable student never missed a practice or a home game. After school he would rush to the field to watch practice or cheer the team on during games. Then he would hurry home to study. Chip was greatly impressed by Frank's politeness and his intense desire to learn everything he could about baseball and being in the United States.

When Chip and his State baseball teammates returned to University after winning the NCAA championship, Frank had been in the joyous airport throng that welcomed the victorious squad. After the crowd had melted away, Frank had approached Chip and presented him with a "mere trifle." The gift turned out to be a miniature tree, which, Chip found out later, was expensive.

Soapy's voice returned Chip to the present. "I'm almost afraid to pick up the box," he said, removing it from the windowsill and placing it gingerly on the dresser. "You really think this little tree is over a hundred years old?"

"I sure do. Professor Kennedy said it was a rare dwarf tree. The Japanese call them *bonsai.*"

"But it's so small. It can't be more than ten or twelve inches tall."

Chip nodded. "That's right. That's what makes it so valuable. According to Doc Kennedy, it takes about ten years to develop a perfect dwarf tree, but he says they can live for five or six hundred years."

"Don't they ever get any bigger?"

"No."

Soapy was puzzled. "I don't get it. What kind of tree gets to be that old and doesn't grow?"

"Pine," Chip explained patiently.

"It looks just like a big tree."

"That's the general idea," Chip said dryly.

Soapy arched his eyebrows. "OK, General," he said, snapping to attention and rendering an exaggerated salute. "I believe you, but you still haven't decided what to do with it."

"I guess I'll have to ask Frank to take care of it."

"Didn't he go home to Japan?"

"No, he's still here. He's going to summer school, and I think he wants to finish high school here in the States."

"He sure likes to study," Soapy said with a grin.

Chip nodded. "You're right, Soapy. But there's more to it than likes or dislikes; Frank wants to be a great chemist."

"I know," Soapy said soberly. "I was just kidding. Want me to drop the tree off at his place?"

"No, thanks. I'll take it to him. You better take care of saying your good-byes at Grayson's and getting that last milk shake. This'll also give me a chance to spend some time with Frank and his aunt and uncle."

"You think he'll be in?"

"He'll be there," Chip said confidently. "Frank studies from seven o'clock to ten o'clock *every* night—school or no school."

After Soapy left, Chip carefully wrapped the box in newspaper. Then he carried the package down the stairs, through Jefferson Hall's deserted lobby, and out the front door to the street. He turned and looked back at the big brick building. Just one week ago, the dorm had been ablaze with lights and alive with the sound of voices. Now it was dark and quiet and deserted, and Chip felt a sharp tug of loneliness. He shrugged off the feeling and started across the campus to the Okada house on Faculty Row.

Chip knocked on the door and waited. Frank's dark-brown eyes lit up with welcome as he answered the door and gestured for his tall friend to enter. "Please come in, Chip," he greeted. "I was planning to call you later, but this is better! Today is my *kichi-jitsu,* my birthday, and a very lucky day for me. By Japanese custom, my seventeenth birthday means I am officially a man."

Frank led Chip into the family room and motioned to a chair as two Siamese cats leisurely stretched their limbs and walked regally around the corner and into the kitchen. "My aunt and uncle have gone to the mall for a little while, but they will be back soon. Please sit down."

"Is it really your birthday today?" Chip asked, feeling embarrassed for not knowing.

"Yes, Chip. Today I am seventeen years of age. In our culture, that is as important as being twenty-one years old here. And I did not tell you, so you should not feel badly for not knowing," said Frank understandingly. "Birthdays are not celebrated in the same way in Japan that they are here."

"Well, happy birthday, Frank," said Chip sincerely. Then, remembering the package he still held, he laughed. "I brought you a present, but I want it back in a few weeks."

Curious, Frank took the package from Chip's outstretched hands. His quick, deft fingers gently removed the newspaper layers, and he carefully placed the box on the sofa table near the window. Understanding lit his eyes as he nodded happily. "Yes, I will care for the bonsai tree while you are gone," said Frank kindly. "I was going to offer last week, but I forgot. I have something for you to care for also—"

He handed Chip several small objects that looked like charms. "These are *ofuda,* good luck charms, to protect you on your trip. They will bring you special luck as you go to my country."

Chip studied the shiny metal shapes in his hand and thought carefully before responding. "Thanks for the thought behind these, Frank. I know you mean well, but I can't accept them. I don't believe luck can protect me; I believe God takes care of me," he said lightly.

Frank eyed him closely as he took the charms back. "I should not have given them to you," he said quietly. "I meant no disrespect to your religion. Though we do not believe the same way, we are still friends, yes?"

"Yes, we are, Frank," said Chip with a warm smile. "We are indeed, and friends enough that I feel badly I didn't know it was your birthday. Tell me, what would you have been doing if you were in Japan? Would your family have a party for you?"

Frank turned and continued the conversation. "Yes," he said, "if my father and mother were here, they would perform a ceremony today called the *gempuku*."

"Gempuku?"

Frank smiled. "The gempuku is a ceremony that is held the day the eldest son reaches his seventeenth birthday. The purpose of the ceremony is to declare him the heir of the family. I am the only child, so, naturally, the Gempuku would be held in my honor. Since my father and mother cannot be here, my aunt and uncle will take their place to celebrate this day.

"Besides," Frank grinned cheerfully, "I know they're at the mall getting me a birthday cake and a present, so I will have two celebrations—a traditional Japanese one and an American birthday! I hope you will join me in a small cup of tea to celebrate."

Frank walked swiftly from the room and returned a few minutes later with a tray bearing a teapot and two small Japanese teacups. The Siamese cats followed, eyeing Chip with some curiosity before they curled up under the end table.

Chip lifted the little cup in a silent toast to his smiling friend and downed the warm liquid. He felt as though he had known Frank all his life—as if they were lifelong friends. "Do you have any other relatives in America?" he asked.

Frank shook his head. "No one besides by aunt and uncle. The rest of my family is in Japan."

"How did you decide to become an exchange student here in University?"

"My father went to State, just as yours did. Mine was happy here and got a fine education. When my uncle took the teaching position at the university, I couldn't wait to get here. I hope to do as well as my father did and also to follow in his footsteps at State."

"You will," Chip said sincerely.

Frank handed Chip a small card. "This is my home address in Hiroshima," he said. "I took the liberty of advising my father and mother that you would visit with them and the family when State plays in Hiroshima. They will be expecting you and will be greatly honored."

"That goes for me, too, Frank. Is there anything else I can do for you in Japan?"

Frank nodded and smiled happily. "I was hoping you would ask, Chip. There *is* something you can do for me, for my best friend, that is—"

"Anything, Frank."

"It is a difficult task."

"What do you want me to do?"

"I want you to help my best friend in Japan achieve one of his great ambitions. His name is Tamio Saito, and, like myself, he is one of your fans. I have been E-mailing him newspaper articles about State baseball. He knows all about you."

"Does he play baseball?"

"Well, he is a sophomore at Keio University; he is on the baseball team. But—"

"But what?"

"Well, he's supposed to be a pitcher, but so far he only pitches for batting practice."

"How can *I* help him?"

"By teaching him how to pitch!"

Chip laughed. "Is that all? I thought you wanted me to bring your friend back with us. There's no reason I can't help him with his pitching. At least, I'll try. I thought you said it would be a difficult task."

Frank's eyes clouded with seriousness. "I did." He paused and then continued thoughtfully. "It isn't easy. In Japan, there is a culture governing almost everything a young person tries to do."

"I don't understand."

"Many customs in Japan will seem strange to you, Chip."

CHAPTER 2

Bound by Honor

CHIP WAS perplexed. "But they must have coaches—"

Frank nodded. "They do, but they are not the same as the coaches here in America. Most young people in Japan are still governed by the tradition of *senpai* and *kohai*. It is difficult to explain. *Senpai* means superior or elder, and *kohai* means inferior or younger. All senpai are honor-bound to help their kohai."

"Something like an apprentice or mentoring system?"

"Yes, except that tradition is the binding force."

"Are these senpai the same as coaches?"

"They are more like sponsors or advisers."

"But the teams must have coaches of some kind—" reasoned Chip.

"Not always. They have managers, but the senpai are the real coaches. A player knows his senpai from the time he is a small boy. Traditionally, the senpai and his kohai are from the same school or town, and the kohai must go to his senpai for help and instruction. Senpai often have several kohai whom they help in business and the professions."

"I see," Chip said slowly. "Now I'm beginning to understand. Your friend would offend his adviser if he turned to someone else for help."

"That's exactly right. The younger generation is breaking away from the long-held, traditional senpai ties, but it is still a powerful force in some regions. It is a sort of paternalism, which means the senpai is not to be questioned about his leadership. It exists in industry, education, and in almost all the professions. In many cases, a senpai even influences the choice of a wife or career."

"It seems to me that such a system would eliminate a lot of new ideas in baseball," Chip said thoughtfully.

Frank nodded in agreement. "That's the point. For example, Tamio's senpai is from Hiroshima, from Tamio's hometown. He was a fine player, but he played first base, and he knows very little about the skills and techniques of pitching. Tamio needs help from someone like you."

During the short silence that followed, Chip thought things over. The practice of paternalism could be beneficial in a great many ways, but in baseball it was bound to stifle the exchange of ideas, information, and improved techniques. It could even hamper a player's progress. Now he understood what Frank had meant when he said many things in Japan would seem strange.

"But wouldn't Tamio lose face with his senpai if I helped him with his pitching?" he asked.

Frank hesitated. "He might," he said thoughtfully.

"How about his education . . . or his future? Wouldn't they be in jeopardy?"

"No, Chip. Tamio has another senpai for his education and career," Frank responded, lifting the teapot and his eyes toward Chip.

"How will I get in touch with him?" Chip asked, nodding and extending his cup for more tea.

Frank grinned delightedly. "Not to worry. He will find you. I have written many E-mails to him since I learned you were going to Japan; Tamio knows all about you."

"Don't the college students have vacations in the summer?"

Frank nodded. "Sure. They are on vacation right now, just like State."

"Don't the players go home during the summer?"

"Of course, Chip, it's just like here."

"Then we won't be playing against the regular teams?"

"Oh, yes! Playing against State University is a great honor for them. Our players are getting together just like you and your teammates. Keio and Waseda are to play a series with State University, and there are two exhibition games scheduled with Hiroshima University."

"Is there much difference in the way baseball is played in Japan compared with the way we play the game here in America?"

Frank deliberated briefly. "You are aware that the U.S. major leagues have played games in Japan. A few Japanese players have even made the United States professional teams. The game is the same, Chip, but there are a number of customs that will seem strange to you. But I don't want to spoil the surprises—

"Oh, one thing. Japanese players have even adopted a lot of American baseball terms, but we have some of our own that you might be interested in. You will quickly understand some of the pronunciations. We say *pitcha* for pitcher, *batta* for batter, *kyatcha* for catcher, *fasuto* for first baseman, *sekando* for second baseman, *shoto* for shortstop, *saado* for third baseman, *pinchi hitta* for pinch hitter, *rakii sebun* for the traditional seventh-inning stretch, *shinpan* for umpire, and *koochi* for coach. And we say *besuboru* when we mean baseball."

"What are the fans like?"

Frank smiled broadly. "Just like American fans. They discuss players, batting averages, fielding percentages, and team standings just as the fans do here. I hope you get the opportunity to watch a professional game in Japan. There is one major difference: We Japanese are a lot more interested in the Tokyo University League than you Americans are in your college baseball."

"How about the stadiums and the playing fields?"

"You will be impressed. The fields are excellent and well groomed. I believe you will play some games in Jingu Stadium in Tokyo. That is where Keio and Waseda and the other teams in the Six-University League play," Frank said, thinking about his home in Japan as he sipped his tea and then continued.

"In addition to Keio and Waseda, the other schools are Tokyo, Rikkyo, Meiji, and Hosei. All have very good teams. You will see flags flying, a regular scoreboard, banner advertising, and fans buying soft drinks and peanuts and hot dogs just as they do at the big-league games here. You will be surprised with the ways the college fans cheer for their teams."

Chip was so absorbed in the conversation that he had forgotten all about the time. Now he glanced at his watch. "I've got to be getting back to the dorm, Frank. Thank you for the tea and the baseball talk, and please give your aunt and uncle my regards. Thanks for taking care of the bonsai tree. And happy birthday!"

"It is my pleasure," said Frank, "and I hope you have a wonderful visit to Japan."

On his way back to Jefferson Hall, away from the spell of Frank's personality, Chip reflected on his relationship with this new friend, the gift of the miniature tree, the announcement of the trip to Japan, and now, the promise to help Frank's friend with his pitching. "It seems like a dream," he murmured.

Soapy was in bed reading *Sports Illustrated* when Chip reached Jeff. "Where have you been? Did you go to Grayson's?"

"No, I was at Frank's."

"All this time?"

"That's right."

"What were you doing?"

"Talking about Japan."

"What about Japan?" queried Soapy.

"Mostly baseball. He told me about the teams and the fans and the way they play."

"You still think they'll be hard to beat?"

"Yes, I do."

Soapy waved a hand disdainfully. "We'll kill 'em! By the way, Biggie, Speed, Red, and Fireball dropped in for a little while. Oh, and the Rock called to remind everyone to bring our passports. He said we won't leave home without 'em! Then he said we have to give them to him at the airport. We're about to be world travelers, and he's already acting like a mother hen—"

"I wonder if I have enough money in travelers' checks," Chip pondered.

Soapy sat up in bed. "Money? That's a strange word. What does it mean? How much is enough? Don't you wish Mitzi was going too? Think we'll get good seats? I hope they have good food on the flight. And—"

Chip winged a pillow at his babbling roommate. "We'd better get some sleep. Did you set the alarm?"

"I sure did. It's set for 4:30 A.M. Rock said to meet at Assembly Hall at 5:30."

"That's cutting it pretty close. The plane leaves a few minutes after seven."

Chip checked the clock again to make sure it was set and piled into bed, but he had trouble going to sleep. Thoughts of Korea and Japan filled his mind, and he eventually dozed off, because the alarm loudly buzzed three times before he was fully awake. Soapy beat him to the button, hustling and bustling and chattering away as he struggled frantically into his clothes.

Chip dressed more leisurely, but he was ready when the familiar banter erupted in the hallway, mixed with Speed's loud laughter. "Hey, Soapy, Mitzi called. She'll be at the airport; you better hurry! And if you guys have more than two bags, you're *not* riding with me."

After a few minutes, Soapy and Chip and the rest of their hometown friends, Benjamin "Biggie" Cohen, Robert "Speed" Morris, and Eric "Red" Schwartz, were piling themselves and their bags into Fred "Fireball" Finley's and Speed's cars, which were parked in front of Jefferson Hall.

University Airport was empty except for the State ballplayers. Henry "The Rock" Rockwell, State's baseball coach, was standing in front of the check-in counter talking with Greg Garl, team trainer, and Tim Fox, State's sports information director (SID) and liaison for the Asia Goodwill Tour.

As Chip and his teammates stood in line behind the three men with their bags, passports, and tickets, Chip scanned their group: Andre "Stretch" Durley, Ellis "Belter" Burke, Michael "Murphy" Gillen, Ozzie "The Whiz" Crowell, Edwin "Doogie" Dugan, Rod "Diz" Dean, Albert "Al" Engle, Jaime "Minnie" Minson, Speed, Fireball, Biggie, Red, Soapy, and himself.

The players assembled for the trip to South Korea and Japan would make up the majority of State's varsity baseball team next year. Like himself, most of them would be juniors in September. Only three of the group, Dugan, Engle, and Minson, would be seniors next spring. Pete "Repeat" Phillips, Hunter "Spikes" Thompson, Hans "Dutch" Carter, and Patrick "Patty" Patterson were rising sophomores and in awe of their older teammates.

"It's a good fielding and hitting club," Chip told himself, "but we're sure weak in the pitching department. We sure could've used a few of those guys who aren't eligible to travel."

His thoughts flew back to the NCAA tournament. State had entered it with only two pitchers, Doogie Dugan and himself, and had been lucky to win. A team wouldn't go far with just two pitchers over a season. It was unlikely State would win the conference title much less make the tournament next spring unless some new pitchers turned up. To make the future picture even darker, Hector Rickard was now gone. The star hurler had hurt his leg just before the tournament and then graduated a few weeks ago. No, Chip reflected, next year's success would depend on little Doogie Dugan, Diz Dean, and Repeat Phillips.

One thing was sure. By the time they returned from this trip, Rock and he and the rest of the regulars would know just where State stood with their pitching staff. Rock would give Dugan, Dean, and Phillips plenty of chances to prove their ability in the games in Japan.

Behind him, Chip's teammates were talking about sports and girlfriends and cars and planes and Asia and the weather and the brief vacations they had enjoyed at home. As usual, Soapy was right in the middle of the action.

The laughter and good-natured joking continued until Rockwell's voice cut through the tumult. "All right, men, we're on our way. Gate 4. Let's go!"

CHAPTER 3

The Friendly Skies

SAN FRANCISCO'S International Airport was jammed with travelers Wednesday afternoon. Although State's baseball players were an impressive group of student athletes and normally would have attracted considerable attention, they were lost in the huge crowd. It didn't take long to have their passports and baggage checked for their international flight. Afterward, they followed Coach Rockwell through the embossed doors of the Red Carpet Club and into a large meeting room with a conference table surrounded by chairs. The boys eagerly eyed the light refreshments laid out at the back of the room, but they waited for Coach Rockwell to speak.

Stifling a grin, the Rock directed, "Go ahead, the refreshments are for us, compliments of the airlines." The sandwiches, fruit, desserts, juice, and Cokes seemed to vanish even before the players' bags hit the floor.

Juggling two plates brimming with snacks, Soapy was the last player to leave the refreshment table. As soon as he took a seat beside Chip, Coach Rockwell began talking to the squad. "Men, we have only a short time before our plane leaves for Seoul. I know we're all sorry Coach Del Bennett's health prevents him from traveling with us on this trip. I know each of you misses Murph too. But we're glad to have along Greg Garl as our trainer and Tim Fox as the SID.

"Tim and Greg have worked with State University, the NCAA, and the schools and organizations in Korea and Japan to make this Asian Goodwill Tour a reality. We're very grateful to them for all these efforts, in addition to their usual responsibilities in the athletic department." The applause that followed was genuine, and Tim and Greg smiled and blushed as Coach Rockwell asked them to say a few words.

Tim spoke first. "I know this is the first foreign trip each of you has taken for State University. The Asian Goodwill Tour was established as a sports exchange between State and several schools in South Korea and Japan to promote education and athletic ties among the institutions and their athletes."

Greg stood and added, "This athletic exchange is part of the larger relationship between State University and the Asian universities. A number of our professors have either studied or taught at their schools, just as some of their professors have at State. Tim and I were also fortunate enough to be participants in earlier exchanges."

Rising from his seat, Henry Rockwell nodded at the two men and began to address the team. "Now that you understand the importance of this trip, I want to discuss our responsibilities. I'm sure all of you realize that with the first step we take on our international flight, we are representatives of the United States and State University. It is unnecessary for me to tell you that I regard each of you as gentlemen who represents everything that is decent and worthwhile in education, sportsmanship, and good citizenship."

Rockwell let that sink in as he paced slowly in front of a large window overlooking the runways. Chip studied the coach during the brief silence, noting his stocky build, dark thinning hair, and sincere black eyes. The veteran mentor had coached Chip, Soapy, Biggie, Speed, and Red during their high school days. Rockwell had reached retirement age at Valley Falls High School the same year Chip and his friends graduated. Like them, this was Rock's second year at State.

"As some of you may know," Rockwell continued, "I've been to Asia several times. So I feel reasonably qualified to speak about the region. I've always found the South Koreans and Japanese to be gentle and courteous people. Their degree of politeness may sometimes seem exaggerated and unnecessary, but it is their way of showing respect and cordiality. In fact, it is one of their most wonderful traits. You will also find that they practice self-deprecation."

Rockwell paused and smiled wryly. "It's a trait quite as rare in our country as it is common in Asia. Everywhere you go, you will receive a polite and friendly welcome. I hope that we can be worthy of our hosts' kindness.

"Now, in terms of baseball, think of this as a long road trip. The majority of our time will be spent in Japan, but I'm sure you'll enjoy our short visit to Seoul. The exchange program covers our travel, hotel, and meal expenses. You're responsible for all your own incidentals, such as phone calls, snacks, and gifts for your parents and friends back home. Just a reminder—be careful with your money. The Korean currency is the *won,* and in Japan it's the *yen.* You'll be able to use dollars on the military bases in Seoul."

Following a short pause, Rockwell continued. "When we get settled on the plane, Greg and Tim will distribute the exchange program packets. In them you'll find another copy of the complete itinerary and several small books about Korea and Japan. Now it's time to head to our gate.

"By the way," Rockwell grinned his crooked grin, "this may not be important, and I'm not sure you're even interested, but as Goodwill Tour participants, we've all been assigned business-class seats."

The players had focused intently on Rockwell's every word in complete silence, until his last sentence. They erupted with cheers and high-fives that resonated throughout the Red Carpet Club. Tim and Greg threaded their way through the mass of players, bags, and chairs, handing out individual boarding passes.

Chip threw his carry-on over his shoulder and, gripped with a feeling of excitement, followed beside Soapy. His thoughts leaped ahead to Asia. They were really on their way!

Through the tall windows, Chip saw the Boeing 747, decked in United's gray, blue, and red colors, parked at the gate. Moments later, the flight attendant at the gate checked each player's boarding pass just before they entered the jetway. As he was about to step over the threshold and into the cabin, Chip glanced out the small jetway window toward the nose of the plane and caught sight of the small phrase, "The Friendly Skies."

A smiling Korean flight attendant, dressed in a traditional *hanbok,* stood just inside the plane's door. She checked Chip's boarding pass and directed him up the stairs to the upper deck of the plane. Chip smiled and received a bow and a courteous smile in return. He walked up the steps and was welcomed by a dainty Japanese flight attendant clad in a colorful *kimono* and *obi*. Smiling brightly, she led Chip to his seat and offered him a glass of orange juice.

Soapy was already seated by the window, testing every button on the seat, a wide grin on his freckled face. "Not bad, eh? Look, they gave us this," he said, unzipping the complimentary travel pouch. He put on the socks, sleeping mask, and ear plugs.

Speed, walking to his seat, did a double take and couldn't stop laughing when he saw Soapy's new look. "Chip, on behalf of the entire team, we're glad you're stuck sitting next to Soapy."

Soapy couldn't hear a word Speed said, but he did lift the sleeping mask just in time to see Biggie, who was seated across the aisle, ominously point to Soapy and then to the storage bin next to him. Soapy playfully put his thumbs next to his plugged ears, wiggled his fingers, and stuck out his tongue.

Once the plane was airborne and they had crossed over and beyond the Golden Gate Bridge, the guest service began. The plane would cross over Hawaii on its trek toward Asia and finally to their destination of Seoul. Before the main meal there were snacks, refreshing soft drinks, and light conversation with the flight attendants.

Chip was absorbed in checking out the flying route in the inflight magazine and didn't notice Soapy maneuvering his way to meet the chief purser on board. Soapy returned to his seat just before the pilot announced, "This is Captain Yeager. Now that we've reached our cruising altitude of 37,000 feet, we'd like to welcome everyone to our friendly skies. Our flying time to Seoul today will be twelve hours and ten minutes. So sit back, relax, and enjoy our special United service. And a friendly skies welcome to the national championship baseball team of State University and their coach, Henry Rockwell. Enjoy your Asian Goodwill Tour."

Reveling in the applause, Soapy unbuckled his seat belt, again hopped over his friend and into the aisle, and took a deep bow. "Hey, Chip, I like this bowing stuff. Think we'll be asked to sign autographs?"

"I doubt it, Soapy, but it looks like Biggie wants you. . . ."

After enjoying a meal, the upper deck settled in as the quiet hum of the engines droned and the passengers slept, watched movies, or read. Chip's small light was still on when the flight attendant passed by with a tray of glasses filled with water.

"I see you are interested in Japan and Korea," she said, noticing the books on Chip's tray table.

Chip nodded. "I sure am. I hope to learn a little of both languages on the trip."

The flight attendant smiled and shook her head doubtfully. "Korean and Japanese are very difficult languages to learn, Mr. Hilton."

"Please call me Chip."

"All right, Chip. I'm Aya Takuchi," she said. "Now, about learning to read and speak Japanese or Korean—it requires many years for most people to learn either language."

"What makes them so difficult?"

"Both have their own language and writing systems. Since I am Japanese, I will tell you about our own language. To read Japanese well, one has to memorize several thousand Chinese characters or ideographs. Then you must learn as many or more pictures of syllables that we call *kana*. The characters make up the nouns or stems of the words, while the kana are used to help with the pronunciation and meaning."

Chip's face reflected his discouragement. "It sounds pretty difficult."

"Don't worry, Mr. Hilton, I mean Chip," Aya encouraged. "English is spoken in some manner or form almost everywhere in Japan and in some places in Seoul. In fact, almost all Asian children are taught English in school. You will only need to learn a few words to get along."

"How will I know which words I should know?"

"I can help you," Aya remarked. "Please excuse me for just a moment."

She was back in a few minutes. "Here, Chip, these two little books will help you."

Chip thanked Aya and glanced at the first book. The title was *Parlez Vous Japanese?* He opened the little volume and found it contained a number of Japanese words and phrases opposite a list of English translations.

The other book was *Your Guide to Korea, the Hermit Kingdom*. He leafed through it quickly. Along with a vocabulary list, it contained pictures of Korea, points of interest in the major cities, a list of hotels, restaurants, stores, telephone numbers, amusement centers, and several maps.

Hours later, while the plane winged steadily westward and as most of the passengers around him slept, Chip had the books open in front of him as he tried to memorize Korean and Japanese words and phrases. Eventually, the type blurred and Chip nodded off.

"We are approaching Kimpo International Airport! Fasten your seat belts, please."

Chip struggled out of his sleep and glanced at Soapy. The redhead's nose was glued to the window.

"Look, Chip! We're over Seoul."

"We can't be! What time is it?"

"It's almost three o'clock. They just said it's already the next afternoon."

"Where did the time go?"

"We crossed the international date line! That's a first for me."

"What about that meal we were supposed to have before landing?"

Soapy squirmed. "Er, you were sleeping so soundly—"

"It's not important," Chip said quickly, leaning over to look out the window. "I just wondered."

Although much smaller than San Francisco's airport, Kimpo International in Seoul seemed even busier to the players as they formed a line behind Coach Rockwell at the customs and immigration counter. "Have your passports open to the page where your Korean visas are attached, men."

The line moved quickly, and when it was Chip's turn, he moved up to the booth and handed the official his passport. The man looked at his passport picture and then carefully scrutinized Chip's face before saying, *"Annyong Hasimnikka.* That means 'good afternoon,' Mr. Hilton. Welcome to the Republic of Korea."

The uniformed agent smiled briefly, displaying a gold-filled tooth, and then stamped Chip's passport and said, "Enjoy your Asian Goodwill Tour."

After collecting their bags from the baggage carousel, the Statesmen passed quickly through the green customs line— "Nothing to Declare"—and out the double doors leading to the parking lot. Outside, a Korean gentleman about Coach Rockwell's age called out, "Hank Rockwell!" and rushed up to bow and then shake hands with his old friend.

Standing next to the man was a Korean athlete dressed in a red and white warm-up suit. Though not very tall, he was powerfully built and looked about a year or so older than Chip. Also there to greet Coach Rockwell was an American army officer garbed in his dress uniform. They all shook Coach Rockwell's hand, who in turn introduced them to Greg Garl and Tim Fox.

Following Greg Garl's lead, the team stowed their bags and equipment in the underbelly of a large military bus and climbed aboard. Coach Rockwell and the men who had greeted him were the last to board the bus, and Chip noticed that Coach Rockwell sat with the older Korean gentleman. Everyone sank back into his seat for the ride to Yongsan-gu and the Yongsan Military Base, home of M.A.S.H. 4077.

The Han-gang River was on the left as the bus maneuvered through lanes flooded with more traffic than Chip and Soapy had seen in all their lives. Across the river, tall buildings rose majestically, forming a modern skyline that towered over the smaller, older Korean buildings in their shadows. The red-tiled roofs of the ancient buildings fluted up at the ends in an architectural style Chip remembered seeing in his Asian history textbooks.

"Look at that!" Soapy exclaimed, pointing out his window to the access road next to the expressway. A white-gloved driver behind the wheel of a Mercedes-Benz vied for position on the roadway with a gray-haired gentleman dressed in traditional Korean clothing and pushing a cart filled with vegetables. "Talk about the old and new!"

Beyond them, on the corner, three women called out and motioned for passersby to purchase the ears of corn they were steaming in kettles over kerosene-fed burners.

The bus passed Youido, a small island and the home of the Korean National Assembly as well as the world's largest Christian church. Chip made a mental note to try and visit the church on Sunday.

It was nearly 5:30 P.M. when the bus driver downshifted and came to a full stop at the gate of Yongsan Military Base. The driver showed his papers to the MP standing outside the guardhouse, the gates lifted, and then they were on their way to the Dragon Hill Hotel.

As Soapy hopped down off the last step, he declared, "Hey, this looks like we're still in America!" Indeed, plunked down right in the midst of Seoul, the U.S. army base was as American as any neighborhood in the States, right down to the split-level houses, modern brick high school, playing fields, and grocery stores.

After a brief team meeting in the Dragon Hill lobby, Chip and Soapy wearily led the trek to the elevators going to the team's rooms on the fifth floor. With excitement dulled by jet lag, Soapy unpacked his two suitcases. Chip pulled open the drapery to check out the panorama of the base below and the Seoul skyline.

"Where in the world—" Soapy muttered.

"What are you looking for?" Chip asked.

"Mitzi's picture," Soapy replied crossly.

"It's in the top drawer of the dresser," Chip said, stifling a smile. "Your side. You just unpacked it and put it there, Soapy."

The redhead rushed to the dresser and yanked open the drawer. "Right!" he cried. "Now I can relax." He picked up the framed picture and placed it carefully on the nightstand beside his bed. "*This* goes where I go," he vowed, sighing deeply, "forever and ever."

"I know," Chip said cheerfully. "She's your guardian angel. Let's go downstairs and meet the guys for dinner."

Soapy led the way to the elevator, pausing at their door to turn and blow a kiss toward Mitzi's picture. When the elevator doors opened, Soapy found himself standing face to face with a pretty Korean girl about his own age. "Hello, how are *you?*" he asked with a broad smile.

The girl returned his smile and politely nodded. Soapy stepped into the elevator and then caught Chip's knowing glance. His freckles merged into a flush of scarlet. "Just being friendly, Chip," he apologized softly. "Honest."

"I know," Chip said. "I was just thinking about your guardian angel."

CHAPTER 4

If Any of Us Can Do It

SPEED AND BIGGIE paced in front of the floor-to-ceiling windows in the lobby of the Dragon Hill Hotel. As Chip and Soapy emerged from the elevator, Speed beckoned to them.

"Come on, let's go! Most of the guys are already chowing down on tortilla chips and salsa in the Mexican restaurant," Speed urged, hooking his thumb down the hall.

The four friends smiled politely at the Korean hostess at the doorway, and Biggie nodded toward three serious-looking servicemen eating at a nearby table. He put his large arm around Soapy's shoulder and playfully whispered, "Behave yourself, my friend, or I'll have to ask one of those nice MPs to take care of you." Soapy rolled his eyes in response.

Chip had been looking forward to eating some of the Korean dishes he had read about on the plane, but as he caught a whiff of the spicy Mexican aromas, he was happy enough to order a chimichanga—for now.

After dinner Coach Rockwell and the team walked the short distance to the movie theater on the base. Chip was impressed with the ceremony that replaced the usual "coming attractions." The audience stood and saluted as an American flag, pictured rippling in the breeze, filled the screen and the chords of "The Star-Bangled Banner" filled the theater. Chip was overcome with a sense of pride and deep gratitude for the men and women who were so far from home, selflessly serving their country.

They were all tired after the movie and gratefully returned to the hotel for lights out. "Get some sleep," Coach Rockwell advised. "Tomorrow is going to be a busy day. Wake-up calls are scheduled for seven o'clock, but with this jet lag," he chuckled, "some of you will probably wake up a lot earlier."

Coach Rockwell knew a thing or two about jet lag. Soapy was wide awake by 3:30 and Chip came alive around 4:00 A.M. The two friends tried to go back to sleep, but they couldn't and finally gave up. They did some reading and then watched the city come alive through their fifth-floor window. They were both showered and dressed long before the wake-up call jarred the phone at seven o'clock.

At breakfast, Coach Rockwell introduced the distinguished Korean gentleman who had met the team at the airport the day before. "Men, I am proud to introduce Mr. Kim Myoung Hwan. He is a longtime friend of mine and the esteemed director of the Republic of Korea's National Council of Sport and Education. Together with Colonel Beebe, Mr. Kim has been instrumental in arranging this visit to Seoul as part of our Asian Goodwill Tour."

The players respectfully applauded the compactly built man with graying hair and a confident demeanor. Declining to speak, he simply smiled, bowed his head slightly, raised his hand in greeting, and returned to his seat. Chip was impressed by his quiet authority. *A lot like the Rock,* he thought to himself.

Next Coach Rockwell introduced Colonel Beebe, a tall soldier dressed in green. He moved quickly to the podium.

"On behalf of the entire base command, welcome to Yongsan Military Base.

"We have a full schedule planned for you today. You have been divided into two groups—Mr. Garl has the rosters. At 0900 hours," he paused to look at his watch, "which is in precisely fifty-eight minutes, you will board two buses, one bound for Seoul International School and the other for Seoul Foreign School.

"You will give a short baseball clinic at your assigned school and then address the student body in an assembly. After that, we have a few other surprises in store for you. Dinner will be on base at the Officers' Club at 1800 hours. Tonight at 2000 hours, you will square off with our Yongsan baseball team—M.A.S.H. 4077—at the high school field. Enjoy your breakfast, and I look forward to hearing an entire report when you return."

Chip, Biggie, and Red, along with several other teammates, were assigned to Seoul Foreign School while Soapy, Speed, and Fireball were on the roster for Seoul International School. Chip boarded the first bus and headed for the back seat. As he got settled, Biggie jabbed him in the ribs and pointed out the back window. "Get a load of that."

Soapy was sitting in the driver's seat behind the wheel of the second bus, pretending to menacingly bear down on them. Then, out of the corner of his eye, Soapy spotted the top of Coach Rockwell's head. Soapy hopped up, hoping to escape trouble, tripped over the gear box, and collided with Coach Rockwell's sturdy frame just as Rock boarded the bus.

"Oh, man!" Biggie laughed. "I *knew* they should have assigned me to that hapless fool!"

Chip smiled. For all Biggie's teasing, Chip knew Soapy's friendship meant almost as much to Biggie as it did to him.

The neatly stenciled sign at the bottom of the hill announced their arrival at Seoul Foreign School. The bus drove around the steep tree-lined grade and pulled up in front of a large playing field. An American couple waited patiently to greet them until the bus doors opened and the players climbed off the steps and formed a small group around them. "Welcome to Seoul Foreign School! I'm Steve Nurre, and this is my wife, Mary. We're from Iowa, but we've been teaching at SFS for about eleven years now. After you meet some of our students, we're pretty sure you'll understand why we've stayed here so long."

Steve Nurre led the players to a locker room to change, and by the time they returned to the field, the bleachers were filled with students—some as young as kindergarten age, some in their senior year of high school. What struck Chip first was their diversity. In introducing the team, Mr. Nurre mentioned that the student body was comprised of kids literally from all over the world. There were children from America, Canada, South America, Kenya, Spain, Great Britain, the Netherlands, Japan, Korea, China, Taiwan, the Philippines, and beyond. *It's a veritable United Nations,* Chip thought.

The Statesmen took to the field and demonstrated various skills: from pitching to batting to fielding to base-running to sliding, and the kids loved it! Afterward, in the school's large auditorium, Chip, Red, Biggie, and their other teammates sat on chairs placed on the stage and took turns talking to the students about what playing sports meant to them.

Sitting in the audience, the Nurres were impressed by the common themes they heard: love of the game, a commitment to honest competition, teamwork, individual responsibility, effort, courage, mutual respect, friendship, a respect for the history of the game, and a willing obedience to the coach's and school's authority.

The two hours flew by, and as they boarded the bus, Red summed up what all the guys were feeling. "You know, the Rock is always going on about how great it is to teach. Well, he just might have something there."

The bus wound back down the hill and through the city, passing Seoul National University and other landmarks Chip had read about in the pamphlets. Everywhere there were stores with brightly lettered signs written in Hangul, the Korean language.

Watching passersby offered a small view to the complexity of the city. Here and there men and women were dressed in traditional Korean clothing, but others wore clothes that would have looked right at home in Valley Falls or University.

White and beige apartment buildings clustered together throughout the city and reached high into the sky. Beside them, smaller homes dotted the intricate labyrinth of alleys and streets that seemed to go on endlessly.

The bus was noisy with excitement as the players pointed to sites out their windows. But as the bright colors of the five Olympic rings came into view, the bus fell into a hushed silence.

The bus that had carried Soapy and the other players to Seoul International School that morning was already parked next to the Olympic Stadium, the main venue of the Seoul Sports Complex, home to the 1988 Summer Olympics.

"Would you look at that," Biggie breathed as the players gathered outside. Chip had never seen a stadium so large in his entire life.

"Come on, let's go," Red urged.

At the top of the stadium stairs, they stopped to catch their breath and ran into Soapy and Speed.

"Can you believe it?" Soapy chattered. "We've already been down on the field. It's amazing, huh?"

The lush green of the infield formed a neat rectangle that was surrounded by a red all-weather track. The seats encircling the stadium were sectioned by color into oranges and blues and yellow and greens, like some large exotic fruit, and the colors were dazzling.

Chip stared down at the field, envisioning the parade of athletes from all over the world, all proudly carrying their countries' flags. A shiver passed over him. *What an honor it would be to represent my country in the Olympic games,* he thought.

Speed, understanding Chip's faraway look, quietly moved beside his lifelong friend and placed a hand on Chip's shoulder. "If any of us can do it, man, it's *you.*"

After a tour of the rest of the complex, the players boarded the buses to the Seoul National College of Physical Education. Soapy switched buses and told Chip about their visit to Seoul International School along the way.

"It was great! That school is unbelievable. It's more like some Korean museum than a school. Ed Adams—that's the man who owns it—has filled the place with antique celadon vases and Korean chests, and there are paintings and tapestries all over the place.

"Coach Rockwell presented him with a special gift from the Valley Falls Pottery—some kind of vase—and Mr. Adams placed it on display in the lobby. He says the kids all appreciate and respect the artwork and that no one has ever messed with any of it.

"And the *kids!* Wow! They're from all over the place! And our hosts were a couple from Texas, Duane and Kim Melsom. He's as tall as you, and she's as tiny as Mitzi! And is he ever funny!"

Soapy was still filling Chip in on the morning's events when the buses lumbered through an open gate and up an impressive drive to the college. Korean athletes dressed in red and white warm-ups, some waving and others carrying welcoming signs, lined both sides of the driveway.

As soon as the State players bounded off the bus, a small group broke from the large Korean crowd and moved forward. A strongly built male athlete, obviously their spokesperson, approached them. He had a wide Michael Jordan smile and hair so black it was almost blue. Chip recognized him as the athlete who had been at the airport with Mr. Kim Myoung Hwan.

He faced Chip and bowed deeply from the waist. "Welcome, Chip Hilton and the State University Baseball team. I am Park Bong Kwon." He nodded toward the other Korean athletes waiting behind him. "And these are my teammates. We are university students and honored to be on the national tae kwon do team. We are your hosts today."

"I remember you from the airport," Chip replied, bowing in return and then extending his hand. "These are my friends and teammates."

Park and his teammates bowed and shook hands all around. "We eat first, then tour, OK?"

"OK? It's perfect!" Soapy exploded happily.

The cafeteria looked like any other cafeteria in the world, but the unfamiliar aromas were pungent and intrigued the State athletes. What especially impressed them was the way their Korean hosts treated them. Park and his fellow athletes led them to tables and asked them to be seated. "We will serve you, please wait here."

Aware of the American visitors, the other Korean students already in the cafeteria line politely withdrew without a word and made way for Park and his teammates as they heaped dish after dish onto their guests' trays.

Within moments, the tables were filled with bowls of steaming rice; *kimchi,* a strong fermented cabbage dish; *maeuntang,* a hot, spicy fish soup; several platters heaped with *pulgogi,* strips of marinated charbroiled beef; and five pots of steaming tea.

"We use chopsticks and spoons," one of the girls offered, covering her mouth with her hand, "but here are some forks for you too."

"You sure speak good English," Soapy blurted and then reddened.

Park laughed. "The tae kwon do team does much traveling. Knowing some English helps."

After the Korean hosts had returned the empty trays and wiped down the tables, Park Bong Kwon asked the State players to follow him for a tour.

Walking from building to building, the players learned that the college was home to Korea's national athletes. Most of them were studying for their bachelor degrees in physical education.

"Many of us want to study in America," Park told them. "I will apply to State University for my master's degree. I hope one day to teach and coach. I want to be like Kim Myoung Hwan; he's a very important man."

As they were finishing their tour, they passed through the main administration building. Trophies, pictures, and plaques adorned the center hallway. While Park was telling the group more about the school's history, Soapy wandered over to look at one of the displays. Scanning the photographs, Soapy shook his head and breathed, "Well, whaddaya know!"

"Chip," Soapy hissed. Gaining his friend's attention, Soapy jerked his head in the direction of one of the cases. In a simply framed picture stood their host, Park Bong Kwon. He wore his Michael Jordan smile and tae kwon do uniform. Flanked by two other athletes, Park stood slightly elevated on the center platform, with flowers in hand, accepting the tae kwon do Olympic gold medal for his beloved country, the Republic of Korea!

CHAPTER 5

Down to Business

THE NEXT two days flew past in a whirlwind of activity. Friday night's game against the Yongsan Army Base provided an easy win for State, and the game was marked by a spirit of camaraderie. It seemed to Chip that the entire base turned out to watch the game; they felt right at home.

Saturday was an incredible day and one Chip would never forget. Before sunrise the team boarded military buses for a USO tour of the Demilitarized Zone (DMZ), the thirty-eighth parallel separating North and South Korea. As Chip moved around the Peace Table and stepped onto North Korean territory, the uncertainty of peace between the two halves of this partitioned land weighed heavily on him.

That afternoon the players visited Itaewon, a neighborhood near the base famous for its shopping. Soapy, especially, enjoyed talking and joking with the vendors lining every inch of the crowded sidewalks. Instead of venturing into the shops with the other players, he lingered on the sidewalks, munching steamed ears of corn and eyeing the shoes, shirts, ties, toys, and belts arranged on the tables along the uneven sidewalk.

In one of the small shops along a twisting alley, Chip selected a yellow silk scarf for his mother, and Biggie spent an hour choosing just the right celadon vase to take back to his parents. "Dad will really appreciate the fine workmanship," Biggie told Chip as his large hands played across the smooth finish of the vase. "It looks like the work your dad used to turn out at the Valley Falls Pottery. And look at the hand-painted depiction of the seasons." Biggie turned the vase in his hand.

"It's really beautiful," Chip agreed. "Whoa!" He glanced at his watch. "We're supposed to be back at the bus!" After calculating the exchange rate and fumbling a bit with the Korean currency, Chip and Biggie thanked the clerk and headed for the street.

After securing all their purchases in the bus, the team attended a special dinner at the Pine Hill Restaurant given in their honor by Mr. Kim Myoung Hwan. Chip smiled at the Korean athletes seated on the floor around the ondol burner tables and chose a place next to Park Bong Kwon, the Korean Olympian. "It's an honor to see you again, Park Bong Kwon," Chip greeted.

"The honor is mine," Park said. He bowed his head and flashed a great smile.

They discussed training and the Olympics for the rest of the evening. Chip admired how hard Park had worked to achieve the gold medal, but even more, Chip admired how humble he was. Park attributed his success to his father and excellent coaches. As he talked about his father helping him train when he was just a young boy, Chip's thoughts returned time and again to his own father, William "Big Chip" Hilton.

Chip's father had been killed saving another man's life in an accident at the Valley Falls Pottery. Before his death, he had turned the Hilton backyard into a miniature athletic field. Chip and his friends called it the Hilton Athletic Club. Chip's dad had constructed a basketball court, a set of goal posts, and a pitching rubber with a home plate. "Big Chip" Hilton had worked out there every evening with his young son. *Park feels the same way about his dad as I do about mine,* Chip thought.

Following dinner, the Korean athletes walked the State players back to the bus. Chip wrote his E-mail address on a slip of paper and handed it to Park. "Write me and let me know when you are coming to State. My address isn't very original, but it's easy to remember," Chip said with a grin. "It's Chiphilton.com."

After breakfast and early church services, Coach Rockwell and the team boarded a dark-green military bus for the hour's drive to Osan Air Base. They would tour the base and then prepare for their late afternoon game with the Osan Jets. Of all the day's events, what remained most prominent in Chip's mind were the images of the Korean farmers tending their rice crops against the backdrop of green mountains rising boldly into a deep blue sky. The game was great fun, but his interest in baseball paled in comparison to all the uniqueness of South Korea.

And, then it was time to leave Korea, the Land of the Morning Calm. They were flying to Japan, the Land of the Rising Sun.

Down below, Chip could see the Narita International Airport terminal. The central building was located in the center of one of the longest runways Chip had ever seen.

Soapy gestured toward the houses and buildings below. "Look at that!"

Off to the right, as far as Chip could see, stretched a great city. The big plane dipped one of its long wings as it began its final approach, and in a few moments it eased onto the runway. At the end of the long taxi, the jumbo jet turned and lumbered to the jetway at the terminal. As the Fasten Seat

Belts sign darkened, passengers hopped up and opened the overhead bins as others began pulling carry-ons from beneath their seats.

Minutes later, the last members of the team made their way off the plane, up the jetway ramp, and into the terminal. The players followed Henry Rockwell, Greg Garl, and Tim Fox, forming a long line behind them at the counter. The line moved quickly and an immigration official with a stern expression checked Chip's visa and stamped his passport as he moved swiftly through the checkpoint.

After clearing immigration, the players followed their coaches to the baggage carousel to claim their luggage. Employees of United Airlines, clad in neat blue suits, greeted the visitors with a bow and a friendly smile as they directed them to the next station. As soon as his bags appeared, Chip claimed them. The customs official gave the luggage a quick inspection before pressing a small sticker across their tops. Chip placed his bags with the others on one of several large baggage carts near the exit doors.

Once the arrival formalities were completed, the players exited into the main hall of the terminal. Even Coach Rockwell's earlier descriptions couldn't match the sights and sounds greeting the State University team! There were hundreds of Japanese students cheering and waving greetings. Each State University coach and player was awed by the number of individually made signs being waved in their honor. American flags were painted on each corner of the signs, and Welcome to Japan was printed in the center. A group of photographers surrounded them, and even Soapy was speechless.

Chip took a quick glance around the big foyer. It was lined with bright shops, stands, and restaurants. Before he had time for a second look, he and his teammates were surrounded by Japanese students who were laughing, talking, and pressing gifts and bouquets of flowers into their hands.

DOWN TO BUSINESS

Most of the young men wore Western clothing. Some were dressed in blue jeans, but many wore black dress slacks and white shirts. Some of the girls wore brightly colored kimonos, and the rest were clad in fashionable black dresses and pantsuits.

At the curb was a large bus with a placard reading Special: State University. The players loaded their luggage and climbed aboard. Everyone jockeyed for a window seat to see the sites of Tokyo.

Chip tried to take in everything—the brightly costumed people jamming every inch of space on the crowded streets; the brilliant colors; the stands crowded together on the sides of the streets; the little groups of musicians playing drums, cymbals, and wind instruments on the street corners. His ears rang with the shrill wail of the noodle vendors' whistles and the constant blare of the taxi horns.

The bus turned into the Ginza, a street that could have been New York's famous Fifth Avenue. Here the buildings were tall and stately and beautiful. Willow trees lined the sidewalks, and the windows of the big department stores showcased designer clothing. After a few blocks, the bus turned again and parked at the entrance of the renowned Imperial Hotel.

It was like an exotic dream to Chip. For one of the few times he could remember, Soapy had remained completely silent. Greater wonders awaited them inside the hotel. The lobby seemed as large as Union Station. At the center of the big entrance was a beautiful fountain projecting a spray of rainbow-colored water high in the air, nearly to the ceiling. It was surrounded by live trees and shrubs and flowers.

The players quietly assembled, trying to take in all of the sights. Coach Rockwell announced that they were to meet in the lobby in front of the bookstore in half an hour. They would eat lunch in the hotel. "Now let's get settled in our rooms," he concluded.

Soapy was fascinated by the sights in the lobby and remained behind. Chip made sure the baggage reached their room. He followed a Japanese bellhop into the elevator and up to his room. Chip walked over to the window to admire the view. The great city stretched for miles and miles, full of great adventures and sights.

A few minutes later the phone rang. It was Soapy calling from the lobby. "C'mon, Chip. Time to eat. We're waiting for you!"

Chip smiled as he closed the door behind him and headed to the lobby. *Soapy's ready to eat. Guess it's true—the more things change, the more they stay the same.*

Chip joined his teammates in the lobby, and Rockwell led them to the grill. Two long tables were set end to end. The food was Western style and served by Japanese waitresses dressed in white uniforms. Chip had hoped the food would be Japanese, but he consoled himself with the thought that there would be plenty of time to search out and enjoy the real Japan.

While dessert was being served, Coach Rockwell rapped on the table with a spoon to gain their attention. "Men," he announced, "you have some free time—on your own—for the rest of the day. Our meals will be served at these tables during our stay in Tokyo. Dinner will be ready at seven o'clock, and I want everyone to be on time. I'll expect everyone to check in by eleven o'clock tonight and be in bed by 11:30 P.M.

"Our hosts want me to present the members of our pitching staff on TV this afternoon. Hilton, Dugan, Dean, and Phillips, meet me in the lobby in half an hour. The rest of you are excused. And one more thing—

"I've scheduled a workout for 9:30 tomorrow morning. You should be just about over the worst of your jet lag. It's time to get down to business," he said with a smile.

CHAPTER 6

Kabuki
and Besuboru

COACH HENRY ROCKWELL and two of State University's hosts were waiting when Chip, Doogie, Diz, and Repeat joined them in the Imperial Hotel lobby. Outside, in the hotel driveway, two small taxis had been reserved. On the way to the TV station, the gentleman who rode with Chip and Doogie explained that television was one of Japan's biggest entertainment elements. "We have the Nippon Television Network, Fuji TV, and Tokyo Broadcasting System. TBS is the one you'll be on tonight. This number does not include the five private and two national stations or the satellite commercial stations now in Japan," he said proudly. "The number of stations is increasing all the time."

"How many sets are there?" Chip asked.

"Many millions. Some people even have them in their cars."

When they reached the station, they were escorted to a small set where an elderly man was waiting at a conference table. Following the introductions, he asked them to sit down at the table. In a few minutes they were on the air.

The interviewer spoke to them in English and translated their replies in Japanese for his audience. All the questions were about pitching, and Chip and his teammates were impressed by the interviewer's technical knowledge. He asked all of the young pitchers about their repertoire of pitches; their favorite pitches; which element they thought was more important, speed or control; what pitch they each considered their specialty; and what they considered the chief essential ingredient in becoming a strong pitcher.

On the way back to the hotel, their host explained that the interviewer was an experienced baseball reporter and had broadcast all the games the American professional teams had played in Japan. "We have seen the Yankees, the Dodgers, the Cardinals, and several fine college teams," he concluded proudly.

Soapy was out sightseeing with Biggie, Speed, Red, and Fireball, so Chip was left to his own resources. He took a long walk, enjoying the sights and sounds and people. The experience was so fascinating that it was 6:30 P.M. before he realized it. He hurried back to the hotel and found that Soapy had just returned. They washed up and headed to the dining room.

Soapy excitedly filled his plate, eager to share his adventures with his pal. "So, Chipper, how was the TV show?" Without waiting for Chip's reply, he continued, "You should have been with us! Man, what a town! I mean, city."

"Where did you go?" Chip asked. He loved seeing Soapy so excited.

"I think everybody in Tokyo was there on the Gen—something."

"Ginza."

"That's it! Anyway, it was great. We took a cab and what a halfback that driver would make—if he ever stopped blowing the horn, that is. And, everyone drives on the other side of the road here, just like in Seoul.

"He let us out some place on the Ginza, the same street we drove through this afternoon from the airport. The driver was very nice, and he wouldn't even take a tip. He said Japan is really happy to have us here."

"How does it feel to be a hero?" Chip teased.

Soapy blushed as he continued. "It's true. Man, you should've seen the sights. Big stores, restaurants, arcade shopping centers, theaters, coffee shops, lots of people, and—"

"Did you spend the whole time on the Ginza?"

"In the general area," Soapy said happily. "In a half hour, we're going to a show; we've already got the tickets. I have one for you too."

"That sounds like fun. Thanks, Soapy."

They headed back to their room.

"You know why the Japanese say 'haro' instead of 'hello'?" the redhead quipped. "I found out this afternoon. You know why? Well, it's because there's no *L* sound in the Japanese language. They pronounce all our *L* sounds like *R*." Soapy was beaming. "Get it?"

Chip nodded. "I get it all right. You're becoming quite a linguist."

"Oh, yes, you're so right." Soapy took a bow. "Here! I've got something for you. A newspaper! In English! Check out the front page!"

Chip studied the paper appreciatively. He had missed what was going on in the world lately.

"Well, anyway, this place is something! Look! Our picture. In front of the plane at the airport. We arrive in the early afternoon and our picture is in their evening edition paper. Read it!" Soapy gushed.

Chip sat down and spread the paper out on the desk. He studied the picture for a moment and then read the story. A headline extended across the top of the page.

NO-HITTER

U.S. COLLEGIATE BASEBALL CHAMPIONS ARRIVE IN TOKYO
Baseball Faithful Welcome State Team

Several hundred high school and college students and fans met the State University baseball team this morning at Narita International Airport upon their arrival from Seoul as part of a Goodwill Asian Tour.

Following the airport reception, thousands of cheering fans and well-wishers welcomed the United States national collegiate champions along the parade route from the airport to the Imperial Hotel.

The visiting champions will play two six-game series, one with Waseda University and one with Keio University. In addition, two exhibition games will be played with the University of Hiroshima.

At the end of the series, the two teams with the best records will play a three-game tournament to decide the overall championship. The tournament is slated to begin with a single game on Friday, July 5, and will be decided by a doubleheader on Saturday, July 6, followed by an evening banquet.

The State Schedule

Thurs., June 14	Waseda	Tokyo
Fri., June 15	Keio	Tokyo
Sat., June 16	Waseda	Tokyo
Tues., June 19	Keio	Sendai
Wed., June 20	Waseda	Sapporo
Fri., June 22	Keio	Tokyo
Sat., June 23	Waseda	Yokohama
Mon., June 25	Keio	Nagoya
Tues., June 26	Waseda	Osaka
Thurs., June 28	Hiroshima	Hiroshima
Sat., June 30	Keio	Nagasaki
Mon., July 2	Waseda	Fukuoka
Wed., July 4	Hiroshima	Hiroshima
Thurs., July 5	Keio	Tokyo

"Looks OK, doesn't it?" Soapy questioned.

"It sure does. Do you mind if I send the paper to Frank?"

"Of course not. I can get more. Man, do I love this city! I was told it never sleeps. Um, by the way, Chip, *Oh-NAH-kah-gah SUI-teh-ee-mah-su.*"

"What in the world does that mean?"

Soapy cleared his throat. "Ahem. It means 'I am hungry,'" he said smugly. "I'm studying the language. Pretty good, huh?"

"But we just ate!" Chip teased, grinning.

Soapy sat on the bed and recounted more of his adventures. "The Japanese sure like tea and coffee, Chip. You should've seen the coffee shops and tearooms we were in. One was called the Shirobasha—or something like that—and the other was the Li Siam. No, that's not right. I guess it's called the Green Dragon in English. Anyway, it has a big green dragon carved on the outside wall of the building."

Chip smiled, trying to suppress the idea of Soapy and Biggie and the rest of the guys in a tearoom, but it was too funny an image, and he laughed instead.

Soapy regarded him suspiciously. "What are you laughing about?"

"An image of bulls in a china shop just popped into my head."

"They *weren't* china shops," Soapy said indignantly. "Each one is two or three stories high, and in the Shirobasha they have all kinds of antiques and pipes and watches and jewels in cases on the different floors. Man, everything inside is classy! There were beautiful pieces of furniture and girls and flowers and pictures and decorations all over the place."

"What about this Green Dragon?"

"It's the best and even beyond that. The stage for their band moves up and down to all three floors like an elevator and they keep playing all the time. And you oughta see the place they call the Albion. It's in the basement of a theater and guess what?"

"What?"

"The music is jazz and rock, just like back home. But the big attractions are the waitresses. They speak pretty good English and they dance all the time, even when they're serving you. And what decorations! All purple and silver and red and orange and green . . . I must have used all my film the first time we left the hotel."

"What are they? Geisha girls?"

Soapy eyed Chip in surprise. "Why, Chip-san," he said, exaggerating a knowing air, "geisha girls don't work in public places."

"Where do they work?"

"Er, I don't know exactly," Soapy faltered, "but the girls at the Albion said that you had to go to Kyoto if you wanted to see a true geisha girl. You know what?"

Chip shook his head and smiled at Soapy's enthusiasm. "No."

"Well, a Japanese girl who wants to become a geisha spends her whole life training to be a geisha. The waitresses were telling us about them. They said the girls start training when they are five years old and keep training practically all their lives."

"Compared with that, I guess athletes don't have it very tough."

"It isn't all training," Soapy said knowingly. "Why, it costs them thousands and thousands of dollars—oh—I mean yen—to pay for their costumes. Some of them *never* get out of debt. I sure hope I get to meet a real geisha. It's like meeting a big star at home!"

They were interrupted as someone knocked at their door. Speed, Biggie, Red, and Fireball stood in the hallway. "You guys ready?" Biggie inquired pleasantly.

"Yeah! Let's get this show on the road!" Soapy said enthusiastically.

The show was called a *kabuki* performance, a dramatic style dealing with human emotions, adventures, and foibles.

The costumed actors, accompanied by musicians, performed on a revolving stage and even on a walkway into the audience. The setting, costumes, and exotic music were all very strange and colorful to the guys. The six friends were mesmerized by the entire spectacle even though they had to rely on their English programs as the performance continued since it was in Japanese. Chip couldn't get over how amazing it was to be experiencing the culture of a different country. All too soon the evening came to an end and the team returned to the Imperial Hotel.

Chip was glad to get back to the room and sink into bed. It had been a whirlwind day of travel, a TV appearance, his walk through the city, and the captivating kabuki performance. But before falling asleep he began to think about the following day and baseball.

Soapy turned out the light, highly pleased with his day's experiences. "*Oh-YAH-su-mi nah-sai,*" he said, smiling to himself.

"I suppose that means good night."

Soapy chuckled. "Not quite, Chip-san. It means sleep well."

Jingu Stadium was as big as Yankee Stadium. While the Statesmen gazed with awe at the massive structure, the same men who had welcomed them at the airport approached them. After bowing and exchanging greetings, the team was escorted through the main entrance to the grandstand. There, lounging in the center seat section, were just over forty Japanese athletes about their own age. As soon as the State players appeared, the Japanese students rose to their feet and bowed deeply, smiling a friendly welcome.

The chairman of the welcoming group took charge of the introductions. He bowed to the State players and then gestured toward the Japanese players. "These young men are players in the Six-University League of Tokyo and will be honored by the opportunity to play against you during your stay in Japan."

He paused and bowed deeply to the Japanese boys.

"Gentlemen," he said, "it is my humble privilege and honor to introduce to you Coach Henry Rockwell and his assistants, Coach Garl and Coach Fox."

The Japanese college athletes bowed deeply to Rockwell, Garl, and Fox and politely murmured greetings. Following this brief ceremony, the State players were introduced one by one. The same procedure was followed with the Japanese coaches and players. When the introductions were finished, Coach Rockwell presented the chairman with a gift from the Valley Falls Pottery and its owner, J. P. Ohlsen. When Rockwell finished the presentation, Tim Fox and Greg Garl asked the State players to present their hosts with gifts on behalf of State University.

Soon, all the coaches and the two groups of athletes intermingled and were talking and laughing as if they were old friends.

Chip surveyed the vast stadium in amazement. College fields at home seldom had a seating capacity of more than ten or twelve thousand fans, but this stadium was much larger.

Chip felt a light touch on his arm and turned to face a young man. He looked about nineteen, five feet, eight inches in height, and about 150 pounds. His black hair was neatly parted on the side, and his dark-brown eyes were friendly and sparkled with intelligence. He bowed low. "I am Saito," the young athlete said, bowing again, "Tamio Saito. I am sorry to be late. I just arrived."

Chip extended his hand. "My name is Chip Hilton," he said with a wide smile, bowing in return. "Frank told me about you. I'm glad to meet you."

Tamio bowed and smiled. "I have read much about you in Frank's E-mails. You are a number-one pitcher. I am greatly honored."

"I'm honored too," Chip said graciously.

"How is the health of my friend Frank?"

"He's fine. But I think he's a little lonesome for his parents and Japan. Do you mind if I call you Tamio?"

Tamio bowed. "I am greatly honored, Hilton-san."

"Good. Then you will have to call me Chip."

Tamio bowed again. "This is a great honor, Chip-san."

"Same here, Tamio. How many people can this stadium hold?"

"Eighty-five thousand persons. Thursday, all seats will be full when you play against Waseda University."

"You mean eighty-five thousand people will come to see us play?"

Tamio nodded. "Yes, they will all be here, Chip-san."

"What does *san* mean? My friend Soapy Smith calls me Chip-san, just for fun."

"It is a syllable, Chip-san. The Japanese use the same as Mister or Mrs. or Miss. We use with first names of all friends."

"Then we can both use it because I want you to be my friend."

Tamio bowed and smiled warmly. "I am very honored, Chip-san."

The conversation was interrupted by Rockwell's familiar bellow: "All right, State, let's get in some practice."

Chip grinned apologetically. "I'll have to go—"

"Yes," Tamio said quickly. "I will watch practice. I have a car here. I would like to drive you to your hotel and talk about my best friend Frank and—"

"And baseball?"

Tamio smiled. "And besuboru."

CHAPTER 7

Tamio-san, My Friend

ALL ATHLETES appreciate good uniforms, playing equipment, and modern facilities. The State players were led inside the finest baseball facility they had ever played in. Their own facility at home was up to date in everything, with tile floors, steel lockers, and individual showers. But when they saw their locker room in Jingu Stadium, they were impressed.

In anticipation of the trip, Chip had kept in shape by throwing often with Speed Morris. But he hadn't played baseball since State won the NCAA championship in Austin. Now, as he laced on his spikes, the old thrill came racing back, and he could hardly wait to get on the field.

Outside, in front of the dugout, he and Doogie Dugan paired up and alternated warm-up throws to Al Engle. Doogie, who was the smallest hurler, had pitched the championship game in Austin on nothing but sheer nerve.

Glancing toward the grandstand, Chip saw Tamio watching him intently. He waved, and Tamio bowed and waved in return. Chip was thinking that physically Doogie and Tamio were as alike as two baseballs; both were about the same height and weight.

On the other side of the field, Diz Dean and Repeat Phillips were throwing to Patterson. Much had been expected of Diz Dean in the past season, but the big left-handed pitcher had been benched because of scholastic difficulties and had not been tested in the season. Diz stood six-three and weighed two hundred pounds. He'd worked hard in the second semester to pull up his grades and had even made the dean's list. For his outstanding academic efforts, Rockwell had brought him along on this trip.

Pete Phillips also was a southpaw. After a successful beginning season with the State freshman team, Pete had been the outstanding pitcher. Pete was five-nine and weighed 165 pounds.

In front of the grandstand, Soapy was playing catch with Red Schwartz, throwing the ball gingerly as he tried out a few tosses with his injured thumb. Beyond them, a pepper game was in progress. Rockwell broke that up when he shouted, "All right, let's hit a few. Dugan, you're throwing. Patterson, you catch. We'll hit in this order: Crowell, Minson, Burke, Cohen, Finley, Gillen, Morris, Engle, and Hilton. The rest of you chase. Start when you're ready, Dugan."

While Chip waited for his turn to hit, he analyzed the lineup. Ozzie Crowell was small but compact, and he played the keystone bag as if he had invented it. "The Whiz" was an ideal leadoff man and crouched into a small strike zone, and he could hit.

Jaime "Minnie" Minson was a veteran. Minnie played third base like a big-leaguer and was at his best as a push-along hitter. Belter Burke was hitting in the third spot. The left fielder was big and fast, and he could pound the long ball.

Chip shifted his glance to Biggie Cohen. The big lefty first baseman stood six-four and weighed 240 pounds. "He's the greatest!" Chip breathed. Biggie owned the cleanup spot.

Fireball Finley in center field and Murphy Gillen in right field were two of a kind: big, fast, and solid hitters. Speed Morris was five-eleven, 180 pounds, and had a strong arm. He made the long throws from the shortstop hole appear easy.

Al Engle was hitting eighth. The stocky junior was an experienced receiver with an arm like a whip. Engle had completely recovered from a jaw injury he had sustained late in State's regular season. He and Soapy were sure to be keen rivals for catching honors come next spring.

The bats were really ringing as Chip watched the hitters. Belter Burke, hitting from the third-base side of the plate, parked two in the left-field bleachers; Biggie, hitting from the first-base side of the plate, drove two into the right-field stands. Fireball stepped into the same box and drilled two more to the same place, and Murphy Gillen banged two colossal clouts clear to the center-field wall. Speed and Al Engle hit solidly, and then it was Chip's turn at bat.

Chip met the first two pitches with a smooth swing, snapping his wrists through with perfect timing on them. Both times, the ball took off on a low, rising shot to the outfield. He laid the last pitch down toward third base and sprinted along the first-base path and across the bag at full speed.

Rockwell sent the infielders through a snappy workout while Diz Dean sent fungoes long and high to the outfielders. Chip joined Red Schwartz in right field, and they alternated snaring flies.

After the workout, Rockwell called them together in front of the dugout. "You were all right today, real sharp after such a long layoff. Our trip to Seoul was designed to get rid of your jet lag and get you used to playing as a team again. Looks like it worked.

"In the morning, we'll work out again. Our hosts have arranged for some cultural tours in the afternoon. That's all for today. Don't forget, the curfew is eleven o'clock."

The Japanese players had been watching State practice and waited for their guests in the grandstand. Tamio rejoined Chip. The serious-faced pitcher was enthusiastic. "State players are good hitters," he said in admiration.

"Dugan was just lobbing them in, Tamio-san. You know, throwing easy."

"You hit balls far. You are a good hitter."

"Not too good."

Tamio smiled apologetically. "I must disagree, Chip-san. You have a good eye, proper mechanics, and fine swing."

Chip shrugged his shoulders. He couldn't compete with Tamio's friendly courtesy, and he didn't want to. He just wanted to fulfill his promise to Frank and help Tamio with his pitching. But first he wanted to get the senpai matter cleared up. "Are you going to be busy this afternoon, Tamio-san?"

"No. I am busy when I go to University, but it is vacation now."

"What class are you in?"

"I will be a junior next year."

"So your baseball team got together just to play with us?"

Tamio nodded. "All players are happy and honored to play in the Goodwill exchange. It is even better to play against the American college championship team. Our university league finishes when school begins in September. We play the second half of our schedule at that time."

"Who won the first half?"

"Waseda won the first half, Chip-san. Waseda and Keio are big rivals."

"You'll beat 'em."

Tamio smiled wryly. "Waseda is very good. They have two fine pitchers and many good hitters. You are to pitch the first game on Thursday?"

"I'm not sure."

"You will pitch, and State will win," proclaimed Tamio.

"Oh, sure!" Chip retorted. "Tamio will pitch, and Keio will win."

"It will never happen," Tamio said sadly. "I have never pitched for Keio in a real game. Keio has two fine pitchers. I am a practice pitcher."

"We'll fix that," Chip said.

"You will help me learn the good pitches?"

"I'll try. But first I would like to know about your senpai."

"He is a fine man, Chip-san. He lives in Hiroshima. He was a great player many years ago."

"When does he help you with your pitching?"

"Only when I am home in Hiroshima."

"How often is that?"

"Two or three times each year."

Chip masked his surprise. In America, boys were coached almost from the time they were able to hold a ball in Little League. Then it was on to the Babe Ruth League, high school teams, and finally college. Then players were coached by experts, even at specialty summer camps. An American player could have seven or eight first-class coaches before he reached his peak.

"Are you sure it is proper for me to help you?"

"It is proper, Chip-san. Many young Japanese do this now."

"All right then," Chip agreed, "but it's your responsibility."

"Good!" Tamio cried. "I am very happy."

Tamio led the way to a small car parked across from the stadium. "Most of the time I take trains and subway—but this is special time. My car," he said apologetically, "is not a limousine, but it does run good. Please get in."

Chip laughed. "Well, it's a whole lot better than mine. I don't have a car!"

As Tamio maneuvered the little car through the crowded streets, Chip learned that Tamio lived near the home of Frank Okada in Hiroshima.

"I am planning to visit Frank's family when we play in Hiroshima," Chip said. "Do you think you will be home at that time?"

Tamio nodded. "I will be in Hiroshima, and I will take you to the Okada residence. They are very fine friends."

The conversation shifted back to baseball, and Tamio revealed that he had finished his sophomore year at Keio University and that one of his great ambitions was to be a starting pitcher for his team.

"I would like to also play baseball for the Hiroshima Carp," Tamio added.

"What kind of team is it?" Chip asked.

"A big-league professional team. Same as your country's major leagues. There are teams in all the big cities in Japan. We have a Pacific League and a Central League. The Carp are the Hiroshima team."

"So you want to make professional baseball a career?"

"Oh, no, Chip-san. I want to play for short time, three or four years. Then I will follow my life ambition."

"What is your life ambition?"

"My humble hope is the same as my father, a diplomatic career."

"But why do you want to play professional baseball?"

Tamio shrugged and smiled. "It is hard to explain, Chip-san. To play with the Carp team would be a dream of youth before my lifework begins. You are not going to play with a big-league team?"

"It's not easy to make the big leagues, Tamio. Is there a good restaurant where we can talk?"

Tamio nodded happily. "I know many fine restaurants." He paused. "There is the fine Sukiyaki Room in the Imperial Hotel."

"I'd rather go someplace where local Japanese eat, if it's all right with you."

Tamio beamed. "Yes, it is fine with me, I know many good places."

Within a few minutes they arrived in front of a small restaurant not far from the Ginza. At the entrance, a Japanese hostess clad in a kimono and sash greeted them. She bowed several times and welcomed them. Tamio removed his shoes and replaced them with a pair of slippers. Chip had a little difficulty finding a pair that fit. However, there were several sizes on the stepping-stone, and he found a pair at last.

They followed the pleasant hostess through a hall and stood in front of another enclosed room. She slid open the sliding bamboo doors made of screens covered with translucent rice paper. Another young and attractive hostess greeted them. She also bowed several times and waited until they removed their slippers. Then, in their stocking feet, they entered the room; the floor was covered with a beautiful matted rug, a *tatami*. The tatami was so thick that Chip felt as if he were walking on a mattress.

They were presented with light kimonos. Tamio removed his jacket and put on the kimono, and Chip followed his lead. Then they sat down on the floor beside a low table, about ten inches in height, in the center of the room. Tamio folded his legs comfortably under him and watched with amusement as Chip tried to arrange his long legs.

"We fix," Tamio said. He talked briefly to the hostess in Japanese, and she then placed a small bench beside each of them.

"Like this," Tamio said, demonstrating the procedure. "The bench is for your arm."

Within moments, the first hostess returned with hot tea. The second hostess was also their cook. She worked over a small charcoal holder on the side of the room. Tamio noticed Chip's interest and explained. "She is making *sukiyaki*. Watch."

The hostess placed a number of pieces of meat, bamboo shoots, onions, and other vegetables in a container over the coals. She added other ingredients and seasonings from time to time, and soon an appetizing aroma filled the air. While the sukiyaki was cooking, the other hostess placed plates and chopsticks on the table.

"Would you like to talk about baseball now?" Tamio asked eagerly.

Chip smiled at his new friend and nodded. "Of course, Tamio. Where shall we start?"

"With a ball," Tamio said quickly. He reached inside his shirt and pulled out a shiny new baseball. "I carry it all the time," he said proudly. "I try all kinds of grips. That is good, yes?"

Chip was surprised by the speed of Tamio's reaction and the sight of the ball. He nodded happily and reached for the ball. "It sure *is* good, Tamio."

Chip wrapped his fingers around the ball and tested several grips.

"Chip-san has a big hand," Tamio said in admiration. "You have long fingers."

"Show me how you hold the ball for your fastball," Chip said, handing the ball to Tamio.

The eager pitcher placed the first and middle fingers of his right hand on the seam and balanced the ball between his thumb and third finger. He held the ball up for Chip to see. "Is this right?"

Chip moved Tamio's fingers a little closer together and forward until they were just in front of the stitching. Then he explained how the key to a fastball was backspin.

"It's an overhand pitch," Chip said, "and you should pull the two fingers across the top of the ball. This will roll the ball toward you and develop a direct backspin. If you throw as hard as you can, the ball will try to rise in its flight toward the plate, and you'll get a hop on the ball."

"What is this 'hop,' Chip-san?"

"That's difficult to explain. You see, when the ball spins backward, it tends to rise. Naturally, the pull of gravity draws the ball down. You understand?"

Tamio nodded. "Yes, I understand."

"As the ball speeds toward the plate," Chip continued, "it tends to rise more and more. If it's thrown very hard, backspin will overcome the pull of gravity for a split second, and the ball will hop a little before the gravitational pull takes charge again. Now, if you were a physics major, you'd tell me in much more accurate terminology why that happens."

Tamio laughed, "I am no physics major." Then he nodded in understanding and flipped his right hand back and forth over his shoulder. "Is this right?"

Chip smiled in approval. "It is right. Now, the delivery a pitcher uses—"

"Delivery?"

"Delivery is the arm motion and angle from which the pitcher delivers the ball. By changing to a sidearm or underhand delivery and by shifting the fingers slightly, the ball will sail, break in or out, or sink."

"It is good to change delivery?"

"No, Tamio. Most good pitchers use the same delivery all the time and try to make all their pitches look the same. They work to get different spins and reactions by slightly shifting their fingers. If they keep their delivery the same, the batter won't know what pitch to expect."

The two players were so engrossed in the conversation they had forgotten all about the sukiyaki. Now, however, the hostess-cook began to serve them. Tamio thrust the ball back inside his shirt.

There was no more talking. Expertly using his chopsticks, Tamio transferred the food to his mouth with obvious enjoyment. Chip watched his new friend and tried to imitate him in the use of the chopsticks. It was fairly easy to pick up the larger pieces of food, but the small pieces were difficult to manage. He was enjoying himself immensely, and the sukiyaki was delicious.

Other food delicacies followed the first course, and then another hostess entered with a tray containing a small pot and two tiny porcelain cups without handles.

"*Sake,*" Tamio said, raising his cup in a toast. "It is good."

"Do you mind if I have tea instead?"

Tamio nodded understandingly. "There is always tea in Japan, Chip-san." He spoke to the waitress, and she immediately smiled and left the room. She was back almost at once with a pot of tea to fill Chip's cup. Then Chip raised his cup and joined Tamio in a toast.

"Chip-san," Tamio said.

"Tamio-san, my friend," Chip responded.

CHAPTER 8

Why
Keep Score?

THE IMPERIAL HOTEL lobby was filled with men in tuxedos and women in evening gowns when Chip returned from spending the afternoon and evening with Tamio. He scanned the big lobby, half expecting to see Soapy or one of his other teammates. But no one he knew was in sight. He hurried up to his room.

He had thoroughly enjoyed his time with Tamio. His new friend's interest in baseball had been intense, but there had been plenty of talk about Japan, ranging across all subjects.

Chip's curiosity about the Eastern religions interested Tamio. The two had talked a long while about the differences between Christianity, Chip's religion, and the religions Tamio was accustomed to—Shintoism and Buddhism. Although his Japanese friend didn't actively practice either belief, Tamio had great respect for religion. He considered it an important tradition. Chip felt Christianity was much more than mere tradition and told Tamio so, which appeared to surprise Tamio. It had been an interesting part of a bigger conversation that compared what life was like for American and Japanese people.

Soapy's voice in the hallway broke through Chip's thoughts, and he braced himself with a smile for the redhead's explosive entrance. True to form, Soapy barged through the door and eyed Chip with feigned surprise. "Well, stranger," he said, happy to see his pal, "are you sure you've got the right room? Where have you been?"

"I was exploring Japan with Tamio."

"That's Frank Okada's friend, right? The one you're going to help with his pitching?"

"That's right. His name is Tamio Saito. You'll like him."

"Where did you go?"

"We started back to the hotel, but I asked him to take me to a Japanese restaurant. We had lunch and talked about all kinds of stuff. It was neat. How was your day?"

"It was great!"

"What did *you* do?"

"You'll be surprised. We went sightseeing. Some of the guys we met at the ballpark showed us around. First, we saw the Meiji Shrine. That's one of the most important shrines in Japan. Emperor Meiji and his wife, I guess you call her the empress, and the emperor's mother are buried there, or rather their ashes are. Then we walked to the Imperial Palace—or as far as the double bridge that leads over the moat. They wouldn't let us go any farther.

"Oh, get this," Soapy exclaimed, ready to unload more news. "You know how the Japanese call someone? It's just like they do in Seoul! They beckon with their palms down and wiggle their fingers. Like this! Another thing. They say yes when we say no, and they read and write from right to left, and they start at the back of the book instead of the front.

"This sightseeing and visiting cultural stuff is almost like playing a game. And guess what? My thumb is feeling pretty good. Maybe Rock will use me in some of the early games."

"I hope so. I was watching you throw this morning."

Soapy rubbed his thumb gently. "I forgot to tell you. We visited Tokyo University. What a place! I think the whole place may be bigger than Valley Falls."

While Soapy recounted the rest of his experiences during the day, Chip hung up his clothes, brushed his teeth, and jumped into bed. With a quick grin he reached over to the lamp and clicked off the light.

"Hey!" Soapy yelped. "What's up? I was gonna tell ya about the rest of the day."

"Practice at 9:30 tomorrow morning."

"All right, all right."

Henry Rockwell was aggressive in his coaching and liked short, snappy practices. Like all good coaches, he was a student of sports psychology and used it in his coaching. He studied all of his players, but he gave his key men just a little more attention than the others.

Now, as Rockwell stood beside the dugout and watched the Statesmen loosen up, it seemed as if he was engrossed in everyone except the pitchers. The hurlers were paired up on each side of the infield, warming up on the practice mounds. But Rockwell had been studying Chip, noting his smooth delivery, the effortless release of the ball that was like the snap of a whip. "If only I had a couple more like him," he breathed.

Rockwell coached and played to win. One of his favorite axioms was: *If you don't play to win, why keep score?* Although this tour wasn't part of State's competitive collegiate program, Rock didn't intend to let anything keep his players from a top performance on the baseball field.

He walked casually away from the dugout and stood quietly behind Chip and Doogie. It was Chip's turn to throw. He burned a fastball into Al Engle's glove. Both pitchers were aware of Coach Rockwell's presence and turned to face him.

"You two look all right," Rockwell said. "How's your arm, Chip? Good enough to pitch the first game?"

Doogie beat Chip to the reply. "I'll say it is, Coach. I wish my arm was as right."

Rockwell smiled. "Good," he said. "Chip, you work tomorrow." He turned away and windmilled an arm. "All right," he bellowed. "Let's go! We'll hit the way we start tomorrow: Crowell, Minson, Burke, Cohen, Finley, Gillen, Morris, Engle, and Hilton. Everyone except Smith get out in the field. Dugan, you throw. Patterson, you receive. Hitters, three hits each and then lay down a good one."

Chip sat down in the dugout beside a dejected Soapy and watched Doogie as the little pitcher tried out the mound and took his warm-up throws. It was unusual for a coach to use a starting pitcher for batting practice, but Rockwell felt differently. He believed in treating all his hurlers alike, and all of them took a turn throwing to the hitters at batting practice.

"I'll never understand it," Soapy said, gesturing toward Dugan.

"Understand what? I'm sure Rock will put you in some games."

"No, not that. I was talking about Doogie and how he won the championship game. Honestly, Chip, he hasn't got any stuff on the ball at all."

"You overlook something vital, Soapy."

"What?"

"He's got heart. A lot of heart."

Soapy nodded. "You're right, he's got that all right."

Dugan was ready now, and Ozzie Crowell stepped up to the third-base side of the plate. Ozzie waited for the pitches he wanted and rapped the ball solidly three straight times. Then he dropped a bunt down the third-base line and ran it out at full speed.

Minson followed Crowell and did the same. Burke, Cohen, Finley, and Gillen went for the fences and powdered every ball they hit. Speed Morris choked up on his bat and placed three beauties over the infield. Al Engle tried to hit the ball out of the park, but his timing was off and he had to settle for three soft pop-ups.

Chip stepped up to the plate on the first-base side to hit against Doogie Dugan's righty throws. He concentrated on meeting the ball, and the steady result was three sharp Texas leaguers in a row. Then he laid down a perfect drag bunt and ran it out with all his might.

Fielding practice followed the hitting, and Chip kept his arm warm and loose by tossing easy throws to Soapy. The redhead was wearing a protective wrap on his thumb, but it didn't seem to hamper his throwing.

After the workout, the team was hurried back to the hotel. Then, right after lunch, the State squad formed small groups to travel along with a number of players from the Tokyo University league. Tamio made sure he got Chip in his car and quickly asked Soapy and Biggie to join them. They all laughed as Biggie squeezed into the back seat, his head brushing the top of the interior of Tamio's small car. Chip introduced Soapy and Biggie to Tamio, and soon they were all talking freely.

"We will go first to Yokohama," Tamio said, "then to Kamakura. This is a nice ride by the ocean."

"I've heard about Yokohama," Soapy said quickly, anxious to share his tourist knowledge. "Commodore Matthew Perry and his fleet put in there almost a hundred and fifty years ago and that's when we first started to trade with Japan."

"That is right," Tamio said, beaming, "but it is noted for many other things also. It is an important port and has many big steel businesses. Many ships are built here. And it is noted for the wonderful dwarf trees too."

"Dwarf trees!" Soapy echoed. "Chip and I know plenty about dwarf trees. Right, Chip?"

Chip nodded. "I told Tamio about the tree Frank gave me."

The leisurely ride along the shore of the Pacific was pleasant, and the scenery was beautiful. For Chip, the trip was too short. But he forgot that feeling when they arrived in Yokohama and took in the city's Chinatown, streets filled with souvenir shops, and the Sankeien Garden. After a drive around the city, the cars headed for Kamakura, which was only a short distance from Yokohama.

"Kamakura is a great city," Tamio explained. "It was the capital for many years. It is a great art city. We will see the Great Buddha of Infinite Right."

"Yeah," Biggie added enthusiastically. "I read about it in one of the books Coach gave us. It's made of bronze, and it's more than forty feet tall."

"There are many famous shrines and temples in Kamakura," Tamio continued. "You will see many fine things."

Tamio was not exaggerating. They visited the world-renowned bronze Buddha, the Hachiman Shrine, and the Hase Kannon Temple. They gazed in awe at the thirty-foot tall, eleven-faced image of Kannon, the Goddess of Mercy, carved nearly fourteen hundred years ago. Afterward, they visited the Ennoji Temple. This temple housed the Buddhist Satan.

Next, they visited the sandy beach of Sagami Bay. Some of the other State players and their hosts had already arrived and were swimming. Chip, Soapy, and Biggie were about to go in the water when Tamio rummaged in the trunk of his car and produced a ball and several gloves.

Chip glanced at Biggie and Soapy, and the redhead nodded in agreement. Biggie grunted, "I'm testing the water. Catch you guys later."

"All right, Biggie. Let's go, Tamio," Chip said. "Good idea." He tossed the catcher's glove to Soapy. "Let's do it."

"Couldn't please me more," Soapy said happily as he stepped off sixty feet. He placed one of Biggie's shoes on the ground as the plate, and the three slowly warmed up.

Tamio was a good student. Chip helped him get his shoulder around in a full follow-through, and Tamio soon began to get his back into his throws. In a little while he was throwing at full speed.

"Grip the ball hard with your fingertips, Tamio," Chip urged. "The tighter the better."

"He's getting faster, Chip!" Soapy yelled enthusiastically. "Did you see the hop on that last one?"

Chip nodded in agreement and showed Tamio how to shift the tips of his fingers so that the angle of the spin on his fastball would be changed.

"This is the same as a curve?" Tamio asked curiously.

"No, Tamio, you snap your wrist for the curve. This concerns only your fastball. With practice, you will be able to make your fastball break right or left. Before I forget, be sure to use resin to keep your hands dry. It will improve your grip on the ball."

Tamio pulled the tip of his forefinger back on the ball and was thrilled by the results. Then he tried extending the forefinger fully and pulling the tip of his second finger back. Soon he was alternating his grip on the ball, and Chip could see that he was beginning to control the backspin.

"That's enough for now, Tamio," Chip said. "That'll give you a lot of stuff to work on."

"I practice two, three times every day, Chip-san. I *must* be the pitcher."

"You will, Tamio, you will," Chip assured him.

By now the sun was turning toward the horizon, and the three baseballers sat down to rest. Biggie and the rest of the swimmers were returning and talking about food. But Tamio and the other hosts convinced them there was one more trip they needed to take.

"We must see Enoshima," Tamio said firmly. "It is an island. We must go. Weekends and holidays it is too crowded. People from the city rush to the naturally beautiful spot. Today it is not crowded."

It was a short drive, and the tiny island was, indeed, worth the trip. They walked from the mainland across a long, concrete footbridge and on up to the top of a small hill in the center of the island.

"We are in good fortune," Tamio said proudly. "Look!" Far away in the distance, silhouetted by the sinking sun, they could see the beautiful and symmetrical cone of a tall, snow-capped mountain. Chip knew instantly they were looking at the revered Fujiyama. It stood out clear and proud and majestic, even though it was far away.

"Fujiyama," Tamio said reverently. "Shinto spirit."

"Wow, Mount Fuji. How far away is it?" Soapy asked.

"It is about thirty miles," Tamio said. "Many thousands of our people climb it now to worship. It is 12,389 feet in height."

"Is it volcanic?" Chip asked.

"Not now, Chip-san. It last erupted in 1707," Tamio replied. "Now it is one of the most famous sites in the world." Tamio turned and pointed toward the south. "There is Oshima; the volcano always smokes."

Chip turned for another look at Mount Fuji. He was just in time. Clouds were closing in on the famous mountain. Within seconds, it had disappeared from view.

"We will eat now," Tamio said, pointing toward a bluff opposite the island. "It is a fine place—Enoshima Kanko Hotel."

The caravan of cars circled up the bluff. At the top they found breathtaking views, a luscious green golf course, and a Western-style hotel. The Statesmen all enjoyed the sur-roundings, but soon their hunger overcame them and they became chiefly interested in food. They were in luck. The sight of the buffet welcomed the ever-hungry athletes.

On the way back to Tokyo, Chip and Biggie were pleas-antly tired and content to relax. But not Tamio and Soapy. Now that it was dark, Tamio couldn't point out any sights, so he began to talk about pitching. He found a ready discussion partner in Soapy, and the two were soon deeply involved in strategy.

Soapy started by explaining the importance of the catcher in determining whether a pitcher had his stuff. "You see, Tamio," Soapy said importantly, with a wink at Chip, "pitchers have to concentrate on the target—the catcher's glove or his knee or his shoulder. That means they can't see what the ball does. They can grip the ball for a certain pitch, but only the catcher or the batter actually sees what the ball does."

The two rambled on and on as Chip closed his eyes and leaned back in the seat. Tomorrow was the big day. Tamio had said there would be eighty-five thousand fans at the game. It would be the largest crowd he had ever seen in one place, perhaps the largest he would ever see at a baseball game. It was almost too big to grasp.

CHAPTER 9

To Win
His Own Game

WILLIAM "CHIP" HILTON took the return throw from Al
Engle and looked once more around the stadium. From the
first moment he emerged from the player ramp and gazed
with unbelieving eyes at the thousands and thousands of
fans who filled every seat in Jingu Stadium, he had felt as if
it were all a dream. *Chip Hilton pitching in Tokyo before a
crowd of eighty-five thousand spectators . . . .*

"Whaddaya say, Chip?" Engle called. "Let's show 'em how
we play baseball!"

Chip motioned from right to left with his throwing hand
and toed the practice rubber. Then he drove a sharp curve
ball toward Engle's big glove. Out on the diamond, Rockwell
was putting the infield through pregame practice, and Diz
Dean was lifting long flies to the Statesmen outfielders.

Engle whipped the ball back to him, and Chip paused to
glance at the grandstand. Female ushers in green uniforms
were moving up and down the aisles, passing out programs
and escorting spectators to their seats. It was a colorful and
tumultuous crowd. White-shirted fans with bare heads

dominated the scene, but here and there, traditional, brightly colored kimonos shimmered in the stands, like wildflowers dotting the desert.

Their practice time ended, and the Statesmen trotted off the field. Before they even reached their dugout, a crew of workers appeared to smooth out and roll the skinned parts of the infield. Others leveled the batting boxes and touched up the white boundary lines. Still another crew of men set up a sound system at home plate.

Chip pulled on his warm-up jacket and joined the rest of the Statesmen in front of the dugout. Then the voice of a female announcer came through the stadium sound system. Four umpires, clad in traditional blue, walked out in front of the plate.

"There's a pregame ceremony," Coach Rockwell explained. "When the announcer calls your name, follow me and line up along the first-base line."

Rockwell had barely finished speaking when his name was called in English by the announcer. A great roar greeted the veteran coach as he walked out to the plate and shook hands with and bowed to the four umpires.

When the announcer called, "Mr. William Hilton," Chip walked out of the dugout and stood beside Rockwell. And so it went, with each player being called by name in formal fashion, until the entire State University squad stood side by side along the first-base line. Then the Waseda manager was announced, and as he walked out to the plate, the crowd roar was deafening. The roar continued all the way through the list of Waseda University players.

The great crowd was standing now. In one section of the stadium, students were beating on drums and tooting horns. The volume reached its crescendo just as two Japanese girls clad in kimonos and obi, and bearing great armfuls of color-ful flowers, walked out to the plate. Then, while the announcer spoke in Japanese, the girls presented one bunch of flowers to Chip and the other to the Waseda captain.

Photographers and newsmen appeared from all directions and took pictures and made notes while the director of the tour spoke a few words in Japanese. When he finished, the plate umpire bellowed the two most famous words in baseball: "Play ball!"

The Waseda players dashed out on the field as the Statesmen trotted back to their dugout. On the way, each player took another look at the enormous crowd; it was an unbelievable sight.

Chip pulled his jacket close up around the shoulder of his pitching arm and sat down in the dugout next to Soapy. It was a perfect baseball day. The sun was pleasantly hot, and a faint breeze stirred the flags above the scoreboard. The Waseda infielders whipped the ball around the horn and back to the first baseman, and the stocky pitcher checked the signs with the catcher. Ozzie Crowell walked up to the batter's box. The first game of the Asian Goodwill Tour was on.

Crowell watched two called strikes go by. He looked at a ball that barely missed the outside corner and went down swinging on a streaking fastball just at his knees.

Minnie Minson took a called strike, a ball, and then sent a hard worm-burner over the bag at third. It looked like a sure hit, and the Statesmen leaped to their feet with a cheer. But their elation died just as quickly when the Waseda third baseman dove for the ball, speared it on a stab-and-grab play, rolled to his feet, and drilled a clothesline peg to first to beat Minson by ten feet. The sparkling play brought a roar of appreciation from the fans. The drums boomed and the horns blasted.

Soapy shook Chip's shoulder and gestured toward the scoreboard. "You see how it works? See the red light? That means an out. Now watch when there's a strike. The light will flash yellow. It flashes green for a ball. I was wondering how I'd keep track of balls, strikes, and outs. It's pretty cool. Reminds me of a NASCAR race with all those lights."

Chip nodded and turned back to see how Belter Burke would make out with the Waseda pitcher. Belter looked every inch the hitter he was. But he could do nothing with the Japanese hurler's curveball. He cut under the first pitch for a strike, took a ball, watched a low, outside-corner curve go by for strike two, and then swung from his heels at a low, wicked curve that darted under his bat for the third out.

Three up and three down!

"OK, Chipper," Soapy said, slapping him on the back. "Go get 'em! We'll kill 'em!"

Chip would have felt a lot better if Soapy had been doing the catching. He had never worked with Al Engle, and he wanted to get off to a good start in his first game in Japan. He warmed up slowly, getting the feel of the mound, the pitching rubber, the field, and Engle's method of working behind the plate. After the last warm-up throw, he walked up the alley and joined his catcher for the sign conference.

The first Waseda hitter was short and chunky and crowded the plate. From his position on the mound, Chip felt as though he were pitching down a hill. Engle crouched and gave the sign, and Chip came in with his first pitch of the game, an inside fastball around the batter's wrists.

"Ball!"

Chip turned and glanced at the scoreboard to see a green light gleaming.

Engle called for a curve and gave Chip a target behind the outside corner of the plate. Chip stretched and jerked the string on the curve. The batter started his swing and then checked it as the ball missed the outside corner.

"Ball two!"

Al pegged the ball back, and as Chip caught it, he heard Soapy yell, "C'mon, Chipper! Mow 'em down!"

Chip wanted that first hitter. He stood behind the mound, facing the outfield fence, polishing the ball in his bare hands. He turned and looked toward the State dugout. Soapy was leaning forward, watching Chip intently. Chip smiled. Soapy always said a pitcher had to get the first one if he wanted to get them all. Chip wanted them all.

He shook Engle's signs off until he got the pitch he wanted. It was his best throw—the screwball. He took a lazy stretch, lowered his arms slowly, and then rolled the ball off his first two fingers as he snapped his wrist sharply to the left. The ball started straight for the middle of the plate, letter-high. But he had put too much stuff on the ball, and it zipped inside for ball three.

Al called for a fastball, and Chip fired the ball straight for the heart of the plate, but it was too high. The batter tossed away his bat and was on his way to first base before the umpire made the call.

The second Waseda hitter was a short, slender athlete wearing glasses. He choked up on his bat and used an open stance, almost facing the mound. Chip knew what to expect from that kind of a hitter, all right. A pitcher had to give that kind of batter exactly what he wanted. Every pitch had to be right in there. With the count at three and two, Chip put everything he had into his fastball. Again his pitch was too high. The batter trotted down to first as the runner moved to second. There were men on first and second, with no one down!

Engle pegged the ball down to first, and Biggie walked it across to the mound. "Take it easy, Chipper," he said, handing his pal the ball. "You're trying too hard. Let 'em hit it. We'll get a couple for you."

Chip took his time with the third hitter, keenly aware of the dancing runners on first and second. Biggie was right. If he could make the batter hit one on the ground, Biggie and Speed and Ozzie and Minnie would take care of the double play.

The third hitter was very eager and looked carefully at every pitch. He worked the count to three and two. Chip blazed a high, fast one, and the runners took off, but the batter was slow. He swung too late and missed the ball by a bat's length. Engle was set for the throw to third, but he was too anxious and dropped the ball. He scurried to pick it up and fumbled again. The batter had tossed his bat disgustedly away, but when he saw the fumble, he dashed for first and sped safely across the bag. The bases were loaded with no one down!

The stands were in an uproar. The cheers, yells, applause, booms, and high-pitched toots were all mixed up in a deafening roar. Henry Rockwell called time a half dozen times before he could make himself heard. Then he got the plate umpire's attention and walked swiftly out to the mound.

"Are you all right, Chip?" he asked anxiously.

"Sure, Coach. I guess I'm just jittery. I've never played before such a big crowd." Chip turned away the second the words were out of his mouth. He was disgusted with himself for making such a lame excuse.

He turned back to Rockwell. "Coach, I didn't mean to say that. I'm all right!"

"I know," the Rock said quietly. "Well, you've pulled yourself out of worse spots. Just do it."

"Play ball!" the umpire called.

The crowd roar was deafening as the next hitter advanced to the plate. He was big, with broad, powerful shoulders and long arms. He glanced at the left-field bleachers and stepped confidently into the batter's box.

Engle looked him over and called for a fastball. Chip went along with that decision. Most hitters in this situation would take a pitch just to get a chance to look one over.

Chip zipped the ball across the plate, belt-high, and the hitter let it go by for a called strike. The next pitch was a curve that missed the corner for ball one. A change-up was too close, and an inside pitch around the knees was too low.

Three and one!

The husky batter backed out of the box and again looked out toward the left-field bleachers. Then he stepped up to the plate and dug in. Chip shook Engle off until he got the sign for his screwball. The batter crouched and leveled his bat, and Chip angled his sharp-cutting screwball toward the plate.

The batter got a piece of the ball, but it slithered along the ground toward first base in foul territory. The count was three and two!

Another full count!

Chip glanced over toward Soapy. The redhead was leaning forward in the dugout, resting his elbows on the concrete apron. As soon as he caught Chip's eye, Soapy doubled up his fist and placed his other hand over it. Chip nodded. Sure! That was it! The knuckler.

He shook his head three times before his husky battery mate gave the right sign. Checking the runners, Chip pivoted and flashed his arm through the same motion he used for his fastball.

The hitter had cocked his wrists and turned his shoulders for a full swing. He started his forward step and then saw the floating ball loop up in a perfect arc. He checked his bat for a split second and then pulled it through in a chopping motion.

"Strike three!"

That was only part of it. The third-base runner had started for home. When he saw the strikeout, he turned and started back to third. But Al Engle's lightning peg caught him before he reached the bag. Chip hurried over to cover third, and Biggie backed Engle up at the plate. Minson chased the runner a few steps and then threw to Engle. The runner tried to get back to third, and Al fired the ball past Minson to Chip.

It was an easy out. Right after the tag, Chip faked a throw toward the runner on second and tossed the ball to Minson. The play had been so fast that the fans were still cheering when Chip tagged the runner for the second out.

The fifth hitter was determined, but the pressure was off now. Chip checked the runner on second and drilled his fastball around the knees of the batter for a strike. He missed the outside corner for a ball and came back with his screwball. The hitter got a piece of it, and the ball went spinning high over the State dugout.

Chip swung around and watched the play. Ozzie Crowell and Biggie were both tearing toward the high fly. He started to yell, but Soapy beat him to it.

"Biggie!" the redhead yelled. "Biggie's ball!"

Biggie draped his bulk over the dugout, stretched his six-foot-four-inch frame as far as it would reach, and gathered in the ball.

Three down!

Chip headed for the dugout, half afraid to look at the scoreboard. When he did look, a big goose egg was just sliding into the lower box of the first-inning frame.

Just as Chip reached the dugout apron, he heard a familiar voice. "Nice pitching, Chip-san." Tamio was sitting right behind the State dugout. Chip waved and ducked thankfully down out of sight.

Soapy helped him with his jacket, and Chip mopped the perspiration from his forehead. That had been too close for comfort.

The game turned into a pitchers' battle. Inning after inning slipped by with the Waseda pitcher getting brilliant, flawless support. The State hitters got hold of the ball, but they couldn't bunch their hits and were held scoreless for eight straight innings.

The fans' interest had centered on Chip's pitching as the innings went by without the Waseda players getting a hit. The frenzied excitement in the stands grew higher and louder as the climax of the game approached. Chip had not allowed a runner to reach first base after the hectic first inning. And when he headed for the dugout after the third out in the bottom of the eighth, he had chalked up eleven strikeouts.

TO WIN HIS OWN GAME

In the top of the ninth, Speed Morris struck out. Next Al Engle lifted a long, high fly to center field; the ball carried clear to the fence, over four hundred feet. But the Waseda center fielder was under the ball in plenty of time and pulled it in for a long out.

With two down, it was time for Chip to bat. He had a chance to win his own game.

CHAPTER 10

Kattobase
Hilton!

JINGU STADIUM was in an uproar! It had been a tight, tense battle between two fine teams, and the fans were enjoying every second of the final chapter. Soapy walked along beside Chip to the plate. "You can do it, Chipper," he said confidently. "You gotta do it!"

Chip forced a grin and paused on the first-base side of the plate. Standing just outside the batter's box, he glanced at the scoreboard. All he saw was two long rows of goose eggs. He tapped each shoe and looked toward the third-base coaching box. The Rock was facing the pitcher, ignoring him completely. Chip breathed a sigh of relief and stepped up to the plate. He was on his own.

The roar of the crowd and drums and horns reverberated around him as the pitcher blazed a sidearm fastball toward the plate. The pitch was letter-high and so close that Chip barely got out of the way.

"Ball one!"

The next pitch started waist-high for the outside corner and then darted down around his knees and across the plate.

"Strike!"

The pitcher took his stretch and fired an inside fastball just under the belt. Chip timed his swing just right and pulled his bat around in a full arc, snapping his wrists through at the impact. His swing pulled him around toward first base in full stride, and he sprinted for the bag, his eyes following the ball as it headed for the wall in center field.

"It's in there!" Chip gasped exultantly, turning on the steam. He rounded first and dug toward second. On the way, he saw that the center fielder was playing the rebound from the wall.

Rockwell was windmilling him on to third, and Chip looked ahead and planned his turn toward home. "Maybe I can go all the way," he breathed.

Rockwell was still waving him forward as he turned the hot corner and headed for home. Ahead, blocking the plate, the Waseda catcher was focusing his eyes on the relay throw coming from the second baseman.

It was going to be close! Fans throughout the stadium jumped silently to their feet and waited.

Ten feet from the plate, Chip took off feetfirst. His slide carried him under the catcher's legs just as the ball plunked into the catcher's waiting glove. But Chip's left foot stabbed the plate a second before the catcher tagged him. Chip glanced fearfully through the dust and up at the plate umpire, hoping against hope for a favorable call.

The blue-clad judge hesitated a split second, and then he threw his arms out, holding them parallel to the ground.

"Safe!" he called.

The fans in the stadium, released suddenly from their silence, were on their feet and yelling as they excitedly recalled the action of the play!

As soon as the umpire made the call, Soapy and Biggie ran out and pulled Chip to his feet. The crowd cheered him every step of the way back to the dugout. There, he was pounded and pummeled by his elated teammates before they let him slip down onto the dugout bench to rest.

Ozzie Crowell was up next, and on the first pitch he drove a hard ground ball deep in the slot between third and short. The play was close, but the throw beat Ozzie to the bag by a stride for the third out.

Chip was still trying to stop the thumping of his heart. He took several big gulps of air and reached for his glove.

Three to go.

Coach Rockwell met him at the dugout steps, his face wreathed in smiles. "Nice going, Chip. Is your arm all right?"

Chip hadn't forgotten that little talk on the mound in the first inning. He had pitched his heart out ever since. His face showed he was dead serious. "Fine, Coach. I feel fine," he said honestly.

Henry Rockwell grinned. "All right, kiddo," he said, gesturing toward the scoreboard. "It's a real big inning."

"I know," Chip said gravely, checking the scoreboard again. The big 1 in the top of State's ninth-inning slot looked as big as 1,000. "I'm pretty sure I can do it."

None of Chip's teammates had said a word about his pitching as inning after inning slipped by without a Waseda hit. Not that they had been quiet or secretive—far from it. Soapy and Biggie and Speed and Red had been especially gabby, yelling and rooting and razzing the hitters and talking about the fans and costumes and everything except a no-hitter.

But the fans in the stands pulled no punches. They knew Chip had a no-hitter going, and they rose en masse, screaming and shouting and applauding every step he took on the way to the mound. Behind him and from the State dugout, Chip could hear his teammates' shouts of encouragement.

Three to go . . . , he pondered.

After his warm-up throws, he smoothed out the clay in front of the rubber and faced Waseda's leadoff hitter. Then he blazed his fastball toward Al Engle's big glove for a called ball. The batter backed out of the box and tapped his shoes with his bat.

The noise from the stands was one continual, deafening roar as the stocky hitter stepped back up to the plate. Chip stretched and broke off a change-up that just missed the corner.

"Ball two!"

His next pitch sneaked in under the batter's wrists, and Chip breathed a sigh of relief.

Two and one.

The batter again backed away from the plate. Chip turned and walked slowly behind the mound. The short cat-and-mouse game between him and the batter was nerve-racking, and Chip was glad when the batter stepped back into the box. He took Al's sign and blazed a low slider around the batter's knees. The hitter went after the pitch with a full swing.

"Strike two!"

The count was evened up now. Engle called for a fastball, and Chip shook him off. He settled for a slow curve and faked a fast, hard pitch for all he was worth. The batter started his swing, slowed down, and topped a big hopper right down the alley. It was an easy out as Chip scooped up the ball and pegged it to Biggie.

The push-along hitter used an open stance, choked up on his bat, and had worked Chip to the full count three times in a row. Chip wasn't going to get behind him again. His first pitch cut the middle of the plate for a called strike. The batter cut under a lazy curve, fouling the ball back into the grandstand screen for strike two. Shaking his head, he backed out of the box to get focused.

The umpire handed a new ball to Engle. The big catcher tucked his glove under his arm and waddled out in front of the plate, polishing the ball in his hands. The crowd noise was deafening. The stands were in a frenzy, with the fans throwing confetti and paper cups and plates in the air. Hundreds of bleacher fans managed to climb over the railing and down on the field.

Chip's chest was tight now, and he could hear his heart thumping away for all it was worth. For the first time since the start of the game, his thoughts were running wild. Then Engle fired the ball at him, and the peg was so hard and unexpected that he nearly missed it.

"C'mon, Chipper!" Engle barked. "Get him out of here. It's gettin' late."

Engle's swift peg back to the mound returned Chip's focus. But it wasn't that easy. Chip's control was faltering, and he couldn't find the plate. The batter watched four straight balls go by and trotted down to first. Now he *was* up against it. Only one away, and the big guns of the Waseda batting order were coming up, the power hitters.

As he glanced toward the State dugout, Soapy caught his eye. His best pal was shouting something through cupped hands, but Chip couldn't hear a single word. Engle had made the peg to first base, and now Biggie walked slowly to the mound with the ball. Ozzie Crowell covered the bag to hold the runner, and Speed moved over to cover second base. The runner danced back and forth and tried to get Chip's attention.

"Don't mind him," Biggie said, gesturing over his shoulder toward the runner. "He's not going anyplace." Biggie held the ball a moment and then socked it hard into the pocket of Chip's glove. "C'mon, Chipper! You've worked hard all day, so let's get it over with. Throw it in there."

"OK, Biggie," Chip said. "I'm all right now." He jerked his head toward the scoreboard. "I guess all those goose eggs got the best of me."

Biggie grinned. "They'd get the best of me too," he said significantly. "Fire it in there, bud."

The next Waseda hitter was broad-shouldered, and his bare forearms were powerful. Chip remembered him. He had struck out once, grounded out, and lifted a high fly to Burke in left field the last time. Now, stepping into the batter's box, he confidently pounded the plate and stared hard at Chip.

Engle called for his fastball, and Chip fired it across the plate, belt-high. The batter had dug in and went for it with a full swing, meeting the ball right on the nose. Chip whirled around and watched the ball head for the scoreboard in center field, right toward the long row of zeros. The runner on first turned second base as the hitter cut around first.

Deep in center field, Fireball was running for the scoreboard for all he was worth. Murphy Gillen moved across from right field at full speed to help out. Chip knew Fireball could move, and he breathed a little prayer as he watched the powerful athlete speed ahead of the ball. At the last second, just before the fleet center fielder crashed into the fence, he turned and thrust his glove hand high in the air to spear the ball.

Chip held his breath as Fireball slid slowly to the ground. Then he saw the base umpire jerk his thumb in the air as Fireball flipped the ball to Murphy Gillen. The first runner turned and sped back to first base, barely beating Murphy's clothesline peg.

Almost immediately Fireball had gotten up on his feet and was walking off the effects of his crash into the fence. The cheers were all for Fireball now, and Chip joined in with the rest. He whooped and lifted his hands above his head, cheering Fireball's efforts. Fireball waved back, signaling that he was all right.

The cleanup hitter confidently strode to the plate. He looked even bigger and more powerful than the preceding hitter. For some reason, Chip's thoughts flew back to the first inning when he had used his knuckler to fool the big hitter for the third strike. Maybe he could do it again.

Engle worked the batter carefully, calling for Chip's pitches to be either low inside or low outside. They didn't want to give this hitter anything good. With the count at three and two, Engle called for time and walked out to the mound for a conference.

"What do you think, Chip?" he asked. "You wanna try to get him with the knuckler again?"

Chip deliberated and glanced over toward Soapy. His pal was trying desperately to get his attention, waving his arms and making motions with his hands. As soon as he was sure he had Chip's eye, Soapy whirled his right hand in a little circle. Chip nodded and turned back to Engle. "How about the screwball, Al? He hasn't seen it yet."

Engle thought it over and then nodded his head. "Right!" he said briskly. "That's the pitch!" He started away and then turned back. "Try to fake the knuckler, Chip. I think he'll be looking for it. OK?" He walked back behind the plate.

"Play ball!" the umpire called.

Chip waited until Engle was all set and then toed the rubber. He hesitated only a second before he started a lazy delivery. At the very end of the stretch, he put everything he had into his screwball. The pitch was in there and darted straight for the center of the plate, just above the batter's knees.

The batter swung with all his might and missed the ball!

As soon as the plate umpire's right hand flew into the air, Al Engle ripped off his mask and charged up the alley waving the game ball in the air. But he wasn't the first to reach Chip. Biggie and Speed and Ozzie and Minnie beat him to it.

They got Chip up on Biggie's broad shoulders as Chip searched the crowd for Soapy. The redhead was jumping and yelling and waving his arms. Right behind him was Tamio. Tamio was yelling and waving a program and cheering as happily as the others. Behind Tamio came the Waseda players. They were shouting too! "Hurrah, Hilton-san! *Banzai!*"

From the cheering sections, *oendan,* came the loud chant, *"Kattobase Hilton! Kattobase Hilton! Kattobase Hilton!"*

Chip had known his teammates would mob him and had tried to get away, but it was no use. He was surrounded.

"Here!" Engle yelled. "Here! Take the ball! The no-hit ball!"

"What a game!" Soapy yelled. "How do you feel? How did you feel on that last strike? What a game! Hey! Where's Fireball?"

Chip twisted around and pointed to Fireball, and the guys lifted the big center fielder up beside Chip. Then Chip looked at the scoreboard. The proof was there, all right. It was big and bold! Nine lovely goose eggs stood in the Waseda column. And in the runs, hits, and errors boxes, there were three more big zeros. He had known he was pitching a good game after that first inning, but he hadn't dared to hope for a no-hitter.

The fans swarmed down onto the field, cheering and yelling and holding up pieces of paper for his autograph. Up there on Biggie's broad shoulders, Chip couldn't sign a piece of paper no matter how hard he tried. He finally managed to get down on the field, and, with the other Statesmen, was pushed and elbowed along by the cheering fans until he was through the players' ramp. Then he was crowded along the corridor to the locker room. Tamio had been carried along with the rest of the squad, and Chip and Soapy pulled him through the door too.

While Chip sat in front of his locker reflecting, his teammates hilariously reviewed and replayed the game, talking about plays, the near-disastrous first inning, Chip's clutch home run, Fireball's marvelous catch, and the no-hitter.

Tamio sat quietly beside Chip, taking it all in. Suddenly Chip remembered the game ball. He was clutching it tightly in his right hand. Then, impulsively, he reached across and placed the ball in Tamio's hands. "For you," he said.

Tamio looked up in startled surprise. "Oh, no, Chip-san, it is impossible. I am not worthy."

"Nonsense," Chip argued. "I want you to have it as a memento of our friendship."

Tamio was overwhelmed. He held the ball in his fingers and regarded it reverently. Then he reached quickly into his pocket and pulled out a pen. "Please autograph this treasured gift," he said.

Chip signed his name. Then, one by one, the rest of the players autographed the ball. Tamio, smiling brightly, could scarcely wait to get it back in his hands.

CHAPTER 11

Face Up to a Challenge

SOAPY PLACED his chopsticks politely on the side of his plate and surreptitiously pulled a little card out of his pocket. He glanced at it briefly and eyed Chip. *"MOH-tah-ku-SAHN-deh-su,"* he said smugly, patting his stomach.

"I recognize the body language but not the words. Can you understand what he said?" Chip asked Tamio.

Tamio grinned and nodded. "Yes, Chip-san. Soapy-san says he has had enough."

"It can't be," Biggie declared. "He *never* has enough."

"Yes," Soapy continued, smacking his lips and eyeing the pot of sukiyaki that was steaming on the brazier, "this is the end of a perfect day. Chip pitched a no-hitter and knocked in a home run to win the game, and I've just finished two servings of sukiyaki—"

"Four!" Biggie interrupted. "And that doesn't count the little side dishes you scarfed down."

"OK, OK, four servings of sukiyaki and I'm with my best friends. *We* should do this more often."

"A no-hitter is a most difficult thing to do," Tamio remarked, reaching into his shirt and pulling out the no-hit ball. Tamio placed the ball in a saucer in the center of the low table. "This no-hit ball has a very important mission," he said proudly.

"You keep improving the way you are, and you'll have one of your own," Soapy said.

Tamio shook his head and smiled. "Soapy-san gives a nice thought, but it will never happen. I am most happy if I will have the opportunity to pitch. A no-hitter for Tamio is only a big dream."

Soapy consulted the little card he held in his hand. "Not when Chip is the *SEN-sei*," he said slowly.

"Chip-san is more than a teacher," Tamio corrected. "Chip-san is a *KYOH-ju*. He is a professor."

"Hey, pronounce that again!" Soapy pleaded. "I've got to learn that one. Hmm. *KYOH-ju*. Right?"

Tamio nodded. "Soapy-san is a good student. He has learned much Japanese."

Biggie grinned. "Oh, sure! But you'll notice that all his Japanese is about food or sleep."

"An athlete has to have lots of both," Soapy retorted lightly, reaching for the baseball. He held the ball up before his eyes and patted it gently with his right hand. "If it wasn't for baseballs like this little ol' baby, we wouldn't be here. And that reminds me. I'd better get all the sukiyaki I can while I'm over here."

Soapy bowed politely to the waitress. "Miss, could I have just a little more?"

While the smiling hostess served another portion of sukiyaki to Soapy, Chip, Tamio, and Biggie exchanged amused glances. Chip took advantage of the little pause in the conversation to note the contrast in the appearance of his three friends. Soapy's freckled face was topped by his red hair, and his blue eyes contrasted sharply with his reddish eyebrows and light complexion. Biggie, the tallest of the three, had dark hair and deep brown eyes. Tamio's complexion was clear, his eyes were of the deepest dark brown shade, and his eyebrows and hair were a dark black, almost blue in color. The contrast among the four friends was even more apparent when Chip included his own blond hair, gray eyes, and tanned complexion.

Soapy was a little uncomfortable by the silence since they were all focusing on his eating. "Er, Chip, did you ever tell Tamio about the strike zone?" he asked swiftly.

"No, I haven't, Soapy," Chip said with amusement, knowing why Soapy had spoken up. "But it's a good idea. Tamio, the strike zone isn't square or rectangular as a lot of players think. It has five sides and is made up of nearly nine thousand cubic inches. Do you understand?"

Tamio shook his head uncertainly. "I do not understand, Chip-san."

"Show him on a napkin," Soapy urged. "Draw it out for him."

Tamio produced a pen and Chip sketched a rough outline of the strike zone on the back of the napkin.

"Note that the strike zone has three dimensions, Tamio. It has width, height, and depth. It is the depth that a lot of pitchers overlook."

"Why, Chip-san?"

"Mainly because a ball doesn't have to touch or cut across the front line of the plate. It can curve around and catch a rear corner, or drop down and touch a rear part of the area. Lots of fans don't realize that and often boo the umpire when he is absolutely right."

Chip drew a line above the drawn plate to show the location of the batter's knees. "A pitch can hit anywhere in the area between the batter's knees and the shoulders and be called a strike. Do you understand now?"

Tamio nodded. "I understand for the first time. This is the only time I have heard of five sides. It is important to know."

The conversation shifted to the pitcher's responsibility for holding runners close to the bases. Soapy joined in, and explained that the catcher couldn't keep opponents from stealing if the pitcher didn't do his part. Biggie then reminded Tamio that all three players—the pitcher, catcher, and first baseman—had to work together when a runner was on first base.

After the inevitable green tea, Tamio drove them back to the hotel. As they walked slowly through the lobby, a clerk in the jewelry shop called a greeting to Tamio. Tamio hesitated a moment and then gestured toward the shop. "This is the famous Mikimoto Pearl Shop. They are cultured pearls. My honorable friend would be happy to show you the many fine pearls. Would you like to see?"

"I know just the person who would like them!" Soapy said quickly. "Let's have a look."

They entered the shop and Tamio introduced them to his friend. The clerk acknowledged the introductions, bowing graciously and smiling in a friendly manner. "I am very honored to meet Tamio-san's distinguished guests. Congratulations upon your fine victory today."

"Count me out," Soapy said. "Chip's the one who pitched the no-hitter."

The courteous clerk shook his head. "I am very sorry, sir, but no. All guests of Japan are distinguished gentlemen."

He turned to the shelves behind him and transferred several trays to the counter. Each was filled with a number of delicately shaded pearls of all sizes and colors.

To Chip, each new tray of pearls was more beautiful than the last. The clerk replaced these trays with a number of larger trays from the showcase. These held strings of pearls. Each strand's pearls were perfectly matched in color, size, and weight.

Soapy was fascinated by the beauty of the necklaces. He nudged Chip and whispered, "Man, would I like to give one of those to Mitzi."

Biggie shook his head and turned to the clerk. "How much does a pearl necklace cost?"

"Some cost a few hundred dollars. Some less. Some are much, much more. Cultured pearls are good pearls."

Chip was thinking about his mom. For a brief moment, his daydreaming got the best of him. He could see himself surprising her with one of the necklaces. He could see the happiness and pride sparkling in her lovely gray eyes.

Then hard reality brought him back to the present, and he made some rapid calculations. This was the fourteenth of June, and they were going home on July seventh. Being careful with his money, he had enough to take care of his spending-money needs and to buy a few inexpensive gifts for his mom and a couple friends.

After thanking the friendly clerk, they walked slowly through the hotel arcade. The corridor was lined with shops, and every window contained gifts of amazing descriptions. There were large silk robes, elaborate mother of pearl furniture, lacquer ware, cameras, wood-block prints, toys, hand-wrought jewelry, samurai and parade swords, dolls, and several fine china shops.

Tamio stopped in front of a little shop window in which some black silverware was displayed. "This is famous smoked silver," he said, pointing to the objects. "It is made from sterling silver with a special process to make it black. Famous Japanese artists engrave it with decorations."

"It's beautiful," Chip said ruefully, "but I guess it's a little too expensive for me. Oh, before I forget, how about a workout in the morning? We're not practicing because of the game in the afternoon. Biggie will start, but Soapy and I won't be playing."

Tamio nodded eagerly. "It is the same with the Keio team. I like it very much."

"Where can we practice?"

"We can practice in Jingu Stadium. It will be empty, and I know the man in charge of the field. OK?"

"Great," Chip agreed, smiling. "We'll meet here at 9:30."

Tamio was waiting in the lobby at 9:30 the next morning. They drove together to the stadium. The field attendant recognized Tamio and smilingly gave them permission to use one of the bull pens. They discarded their coats and slipped quickly into their spikes. Soapy had brought his own glove and took the catcher's position behind the practice plate while Tamio and Chip alternated throws from the pitching rubber.

Chip watched Tamio's pitching motion closely. The younger hurler weighed only 150 pounds, but he got a lot of speed out of his throws. Chip spotted his first weakness quickly: All of Tamio's throws were made solely with his arm. He had forgotten Chip's earlier emphasis on using a full-arm swing along with the full use of his body. But before Chip could say anything, Tamio remembered and apologized.

"Please excuse me, Chip-san. I forgot to use my shoulder and back. I will not make this mistake again."

After half an hour of easy throwing and working on Tamio's form, Chip taught him to lift his fingertips and grip the ball with his thumb and little finger. "Watch the forward spin, Tamio."

After several throws, Tamio nodded eagerly. "It is good. It is a new pitch."

Chip then showed Tamio why it was important to swing his arm in a big arc and, at the same time, hide the ball. "Keep the ball hidden in your glove as long as possible, and when you drop your glove away from the ball, try to shield it with your leg and body."

Chip demonstrated in slow motion, and Tamio imitated him. "Now for a change of pace. Do a change-up with the same motion," Chip suggested.

Tamio tried it over and over again until he got the idea. Chip smiled his approval. Then they worked on a floater. Chip taught Tamio to place the fingernails of his first, second, and third fingers behind the ball and to grip it with his thumb and little finger. After several throws, Tamio nodded eagerly. "It is good!"

"You're making wonderful progress," Chip said enthusiastically.

"How about working on his control, Chip?" Soapy called.

"Good idea."

Soapy assumed his regular catcher's stance and moved his glove from one spot to another as Tamio tried to drive the ball to the exact position of Soapy's glove. After a few throws, Chip began to call the pitches. Tamio responded with perfectly placed control.

"The Keio catchers never change the position of the glove," Tamio said wistfully. "They stand like this." He demonstrated.

"I know. Most catchers don't. That's why Soapy is so valuable," Chip said.

"How does he know where I will throw the ball?" Tamio asked.

Chip smiled. "Don't you remember what Soapy was telling you when we were coming back from Yokohama and Kamakura in the car?" he asked teasingly.

Tamio nodded quickly. "Yes, I must try to throw the ball at the catcher's knee or shoulder or head. Is this right?"

"Yes," Chip replied, smiling. "Try a few. Ready, Soapy?"

Soapy nodded and assumed his position. He held his glove and throwing hand directly behind the center of the plate and called out the target for each of Tamio's throws: "Right knee, left knee, right shoulder, left shoulder."

Tamio soon was nodding with satisfaction as his pitches began to find the targets Soapy called. After a few throws, they sat down for a break. Tamio had proved to be a good student. He looked questioningly at Chip. "Am I a bad pitcher?"

"Bad!" Soapy echoed indignantly. "Why, you're as good as—as good as Doogie Dugan! And he's good enough to pitch against *your* school this afternoon."

Tamio eyed his two friends. "I am very grateful. I have learned more in just two days than in my whole life. I can never repay you."

"You just work on the stuff Chip is teaching you, and you'll be a first-class pitcher," Soapy said stoutly.

"Is this so, Chip-san?"

"It is so," Chip said firmly. "If you practice every day for two weeks as you did this morning, you will be ready to pitch for *any* college team."

Tamio's face brightened. "I can do it," he promised. "No, Chip-san, sorry. I *must* do it."

Chip and Soapy exchanged a long glance. They liked people who could face up to a challenge. They knew what a driving urge could accomplish if a person never let down and never let discouragement get to him. In unison, almost as if by signal, they turned toward their new friend and nodded approvingly.

Tamio probably didn't realize it, and it's unlikely that Chip and Soapy gave it any conscious thought either. But right then a warm and lasting friendship was welded among the three.

CHAPTER 12

The Fine Art of Baseball

CHIP AND SOAPY sat side by side in the State dugout in Jingu Stadium that afternoon and watched Tamio pitch for the Keio University batting practice. The Japanese pitcher's progress was clearly evident both in the way he concealed the ball from the hitters and in the full sweep of his arm.

"He's practicing everything you taught him, Chip," Soapy said, nodding toward the mound. "I hope his coach or manager or sen—what did you say they called those guys?"

"Senpai."

"Well, I hope he realizes it."

"I doubt it," Chip said thoughtfully. "You know what it's like to pitch for batting practice. You can't use any stuff and you have to put every pitch right over the center of the plate."

When the Keio batting practice was over, the State players ran out on the field for their infield practice. Tamio glanced over at Chip and Soapy and waved. Then he continued toward the Keio bull pen.

NO-HITTER

Al Engle warmed up Doogie Dugan in front of the State University dugout, and Chip and Soapy played catch. When the fielding practice was over, Rockwell sent Chip, Soapy, Patty Patterson, Diz Dean, and Repeat Phillips out to the State bull pen.

"Have Dean ready to pitch for batting practice, Patterson," Rockwell called. Diz Dean was clearly disappointed. "I hope I get a chance to start a game on this trip," he muttered bitterly.

"There's lots of time, Diz," Chip said gently. "After all, Doogie deserves to start this game. In fact, he should have started yesterday."

"Who are you kidding, Chip?" Dean argued. "He wins one game and he's a hero?"

"It meant the championship," Chip said quietly.

"How about me?" Soapy interrupted, examining his thumb.

"And me," Pete Phillips added. "I'll be lucky to get a chance to pitch batting practice."

"Don't worry, Repeat. We'll all get a turn at that," Chip said cheerfully. "I'm sure you'll see some action."

"Well," Patty Patterson concluded, "I'm the number-one bull-pen receiver."

That afternoon, State had first turn at bat, and the Keio pitcher proved to be just as good as Tamio had said. He sent Crowell, Minson, and Burke down one-two-three!

Doogie Dugan had gotten off to a slow start in the past season, mostly because Chip and Hector "Hex" Rickard, State's star senior pitcher, had worked every game on the schedule. However, in the NCAA semifinal and final games, Rickard had been injured. Chip had pitched the team to victory in the semifinal game, and Dugan had pitched the final game, winning the championship for State University.

Today he was in trouble from the very first inning. The first Keio batter bunted safely, and the number-two hitter laid down a perfect sacrifice bunt that advanced the runner to second. The third batter doubled to the right-field fence, causing the runner on second to score. The cleanup batter teed off and laced one over the right-field fence, scoring the second-base runner as well as himself. The home run upset Dugan, and he walked the next batter.

Then he got a break. On a hit and run, the batter lined to Crowell. The little keystone whiz made a double play, sending the runner on first back to the dugout to retire the side. The score: Keio 3, State 0.

The Statesmen got one run back in the top of the second and another in the third. But, to the joy of the thousands of fans who jammed the stadium, Keio came back in the bottom of the third to score two more runs to lead 5-2.

It was that kind of game right through to the bottom of the seventh. With State trailing by two runs, 9-7, and no one out, Keio loaded the bases on a walk and two singles. From the top step of the dugout, Coach Rockwell called, "Time!"

Patterson had Diz Dean ready, and Rockwell waved him in from the bull pen. Before Diz could put out the fire, two more runs were scored. When State came to bat in the top of the eighth, Keio was leading 11-7.

The Keio starting pitcher had gone all the way. Now, the big end of the State batting order was up, and it was clear the pressure of State's bats was beginning to tell. The Keio pitcher walked Crowell and Minson, and that brought out the Keio manager. Like Rockwell, he called for time and waved in another pitcher.

While the Keio manager was holding an infield conference, Rockwell yelled for Chip. Chip trotted in from the bull pen to hit for Burke. The Rock walked in from the third-base coaching box to meet him in front of the bat rack.

"We'll try the hit and run, Chip," Rockwell said seriously. "It's risky, but we're down four runs and running out of innings. I'll put the play on with our signs. You know your job—try to hit behind the runners. You'd better hit lefty. All right?"

Chip got his bat and waited until the relief pitcher finished his warm-up throws. As he walked slowly to the first-base side of the plate, the crowd gave him a tremendous round of applause.

The pitcher checked Crowell and Minson on first and second and then fed Chip a good bunting ball, low and inside. Chip let it go by and breathed a sigh of relief when the umpire called it a ball. He backed out of the box and glanced at Coach Rockwell. The coach had cupped his hands over his mouth and was yelling something across the infield to Minson. But Chip noted that the tips of Rockwell's shoes were lined up squarely on the coaching-box line directly opposite third base. The hit and run was on.

The pitcher came in with a fastball just above his knees, and Chip golfed it over first base in a perfect hit-and-run execution. The hit was good for two bases, and Crowell scored. Minson held up at third. Again, Chip got a tremendous round of applause from the stands.

Biggie Cohen was up now. The pitcher fed his catcher four pitchouts, evidently under orders to put State's powerful cleanup hitter on base. The bases were loaded as Fireball Finley tapped his bat on the ground, dropped the warm-up batting doughnut, and strode to the plate.

Fireball batted from the first-base side of the plate and had gone two for three so far in the game. He took a ball and a called strike before lifting a high fly to right field. As soon as the fielder camped under the ball, Minson, Chip, and Biggie tagged up.

Minson scored, Chip made it to third, and Biggie held up on second. They were one down. A hit could tie the score. Murphy Gillen tried, but the best he could do was a high fly to left field.

"Tag up, Chip," Rockwell cried.

Chip tagged up and sprinted for home as soon as he heard Rockwell's "Go!" He knew it would be close—the throw would be right on his heels. He didn't take any chances. Chip hit the dirt and slid across the plate just before the catcher made the tag.

Biggie was now perched on third base. State had a big rally going, and it suddenly looked bad for Keio. But Speed's hard-hit grounder to third base resulted in an easy out at first. The score at the end of the State half of the eighth was Keio 11, State 10.

Diz Dean's pitching was wild but effective. His tremendous speed was too much for the Keio batters in the bottom of the eighth, and he practically blasted away the three men who faced him. That brought State in for their last licks—their last chance to win the game.

The Keio pitcher worked carefully and got Engle on a high infield fly. He set Diz Dean down in short order, getting the big lefty with three straight curveballs. Ozzie Crowell was up next and kept the Statesmen's hopes alive by beating out a grass cutter to deep short.

Next up, Minson met the first pitch squarely on the nose, but the ball headed straight for the left fielder, who waited for the catch and gathered in the ball for the third out.

Keio had survived State's late-inning rally, winning 11-10.

Soapy dragged in from the bull pen, looking quite sad. Chip waited for him on the ramp leading to the locker room. "We'll kill 'em," Chip said significantly.

"You've got to have pitching in *any* league," Soapy said sourly. "I didn't see Waseda scoring eleven runs yesterday."

"How about us? How many runs did we get?"

"Well, anyway," Soapy said weakly, "we won."

"And *they* won today," Chip concluded. "We've got to face it, Soapy. They're both good teams, and we're going to have a tough time winning either one of the series. Oh—

"I almost forgot. Tamio said he would wait for us after the game. Let's get moving. And don't forget to congratulate him on the Keio victory."

"It seems almost like congratulating a teammate," Soapy said thoughtfully.

Chip nodded. "You're right. He does seem like a teammate."

After Coach Rockwell's postgame meeting, Chip and Soapy showered quickly and hurried out the main entrance. Tamio was sitting on the hood of his car across the street and waved to them.

"Nice win, Tamio-san," Chip said.

"Me, too," Soapy added. "Keio was too tough for us today."

Tamio smiled. "It was a fine game. Where is Biggie-san?"

"He said he'd catch us next time; he had something to do with Speed," Soapy explained, staring intently through the window of the restaurant next door.

"Chip-san, do you like our Keio pitchers?"

"They were very good, Tamio," Chip said, "but you're just as good. Better!"

"Hey, Chip!" Soapy interrupted. "I've got a great idea! Why don't we give Tamio a baseball test?"

Chip nodded. "Sure. Where?"

"Well," Soapy reflected, "we should find some establishment where the examinee—ahem—would feel at ease. How about a little sukiyaki place?"

"Sukiyaki!" Chip and Tamio chorused, grinning at the same time.

"Good, that's settled," Soapy said quickly. "Not that we'll let the sukiyaki interfere with the baseball test—"

"Naturally," Chip said knowingly.

"It is a good idea," Tamio said cheerfully. "First, I would like to take you two friends on a little drive to see more sights."

Tamio drove skillfully through the busy, congested city and then up a hill. "This is Kudan Hill," he explained. "Shokonsha is a shrine for warriors who have given their lives for Japan. The emperor visits often to pay his respect to these heroes."

They walked through the compound, and putting on slippers, passed through the outer shrine to a point where they could gaze at the door of the inner shrine.

"This small house has a casket with names of many famous Japanese soldiers," Tamio said.

After spending a few minutes there, they visited the shrine's military museum, which was filled with war relics. A special exhibit displayed all different types of Japanese weapons arranged in chronological order from ancient times. Chip was especially fascinated by the samurai armor-clad warrior from the Kamakura period. It was interesting, but Soapy was getting restless and hungry, so they headed for Tamio's favorite sukiyaki restaurant.

Soapy reached for the menu as soon as he sat down at the table, leaving Chip to take charge of the baseball questioning. "How does the pitcher hold the ball?"

Tamio reached inside his shirt and pulled out the no-hit ball. He held it up for Chip to see. "You like?"

"Absolutely!" Chip said. "It's great!"

The autographs of the players had been traced over with heavy, black ink, and then the ball had been lacquered. No-Hitter Ball and the date were written on it in larger letters. He placed his fingers correctly on the seams and held the ball up for Chip to see. "Is this right?"

"Right! Do you grip the ball tightly?"

Tamio nodded. "Yes, I must hold it very tight with my fingertips, Chip-san."

"How does the pitcher put spin on the ball?"

"By the way he releases it from his fingers, Chip-san."

"What does spin do to the ball?"

"It makes the ball spin to the sides or hop or drop down toward the plate."

Chip was pleased with his friend's answers and nodded. "Now, Tamio-san," he said slowly, "there is something else that makes the ball curve. What is it?"

"The seams on the ball, Chip-san. The seams make a whirlpool of air around the ball. The air pressure on the side that the ball spins on is lower than the other side. The ball breaks that way."

Chip grinned and glanced at Soapy, "All right?"

Soapy had a mouthful of *shumai*—a shrimp dumpling he had ordered as an appetizer—but he paused long enough to nod enthusiastically. "Very good!" he gulped. "Now he's doing the teaching. Where did you learn about the seams, Tamio-san?" Soapy asked as another shumai disappeared.

"I read in an American paper about it, Soapy-san. An American scientist did a test. He found the ball breaks eleven inches when the pitcher throws the ball one hundred feet per second. In sixty feet, if the ball has much spin and twelve hundred RPM, the ball will curve eleven inches. Also, if the pitcher can spin the ball eighteen hundred RPM, the ball will curve more than seventeen inches."

Still chewing, Soapy lifted his eyebrows and nodded in awe.

Chip resumed the questioning. "What makes backspin?"

"The grip on the ball, Chip-san. The two first fingers are the last to leave the ball with hard throws and so the ball spins backward."

Soapy pushed his empty plate away and joined in the questioning. "What is meant by the pitcher's delivery?"

"It is the way a pitcher swings his arm and throws the ball, Soapy-san."

"Are there different kinds of deliveries?"

"Yes, Soapy-san, many kinds. But Chip-san says good pitchers try to make all their pitches look alike."

"How does a pitcher get different kinds of spin on the ball?"

Tamio showed how to pull one finger behind the other to impart certain kinds of spin and how to use a wrist-snap to gain greater spin. Chip and Soapy were both impressed with Tamio's quick responses.

Then Soapy quizzed him about the strike zone and the techniques the pitcher used to hold runners close to the bases. When he finished, he shook his head in admiration and glanced at Chip.

"He's sure got it down perfect!" He turned back to Tamio. "Young man," Soapy said pompously, rising to his feet, "it is my privilege to recommend you to the dean of the graduate school for a Ph.D. in the fine art of baseball. Congratulations. To celebrate this auspicious distinction, let's order some tempura."

CHAPTER 13

Tamio's Honorable Friends

CHIP WAS glad to get back to the hotel. So much had happened during the past ten days: the trip to Korea, the clinics with school children, the Olympic Stadium, flying to Japan, going to practice, playing two games. He was tired of excitement and crowds and sightseeing. All he wanted to do was write a few E-mails in the hotel's business center and relax. But not Soapy! The redhead thrived on action.

"Come on, Chipper. I want to see how the Japanese big-league teams play. Especially under lights."

"I'm worn out, Soapy. Besides, I promised Tamio I'd wait for him."

"Do you mind if I go? Some of the guys are ready. But I'll stay—"

"No, Soapy. Go ahead. You can give me the play-by-play when you get back. I'll send some E-mails and tell everybody you're out devouring Tokyo."

"Great! Can you send one to Mitzi from both of us?" Soapy called as he left.

After Soapy was gone, Chip took the elevator to the third floor and pulled open the double glass doors to the ornately decorated Imperial Hotel Business Center. The young woman behind the desk bowed and then escorted Chip to a small office. Chip thanked her and settled into the thick leather chair facing the computer screen.

He logged on and checked his E-mail account for incoming messages, and then spent the next hour writing his mom and some friends from Valley Falls: Taps Browning, Doc Jones, Mr. Schroeder, and Petey Jackson at the Sugar Bowl.

Next his thoughts turned to University. He wrote to Mr. Grayson, Whitty Whittemore, and Mitzi Savrill, with special regards from Soapy. His E-mail to Frank Okada about Japan, baseball, and Tamio was the longest message he sent. Before reading the online newspapers in Valley Falls and University, Chip sent an E-mail to Peggy Armstrong.

He had just returned to his room when the phone rang. It was Tamio.

"Chip-san! This is Tamio. Can you and Soapy-san join me and two honorable friends for some nice food and a visit?"

"Sure, I guess so, Tamio-san. But Soapy's gone to the Tokyo Dome with some of the guys to watch a game."

"Soapy-san will have a good time. The restaurant is one block away, Chip-san. These friends are very important persons. They admire you very much. We will stay only a short time. It is important to me, Chip-san. Please."

Chip reluctantly agreed and joined Tamio in the lobby. It was only a short walk to the restaurant, and beginning with the stepping-stone at the entrance, Chip sensed that this restaurant was very special.

Their kimono-clad hostess greeted them in a good-sized central room surrounded by a number of smaller rooms, but Chip was surprised to notice that none were occupied. He followed Tamio and the hostess to another door. She slid back the rice paper doors to reveal a magnificent rock garden bordered by several trees on the outer edges. Across from the garden was their destination, a small private room.

Chip and Tamio traded their shoes for slippers at the door and removed these just before entering the small, tatami-matted tearoom. At the door the hostess provided them with expensively brocaded kimonos and took their coats. A young Japanese couple dressed in Western clothing was seated at the low table in the room. The young man immediately rose and bowed.

Tamio bowed several times in return. He introduced them as honorable friends and waited until his American friend had seated himself. Then he pointed to a cushion on the floor. "*Zabuton,*" he explained, "to sit down on."

Chip sat down on the zabuton and tried to look comfortable. Gazing through the open rice-paper door, Chip remarked, "This is very peaceful. Thank you for inviting me."

As the hostess served green tea and cookies, Tamio's friend responded, "Thank you, Mr. Hilton. Our traditional Japanese gardens focus on nature and convey tranquility. This garden is an arrangement of shapes and textures modeled after the garden at the Ryoanji Temple in Kyoto."

After a polite pause, Tamio began to talk baseball, explaining that his friends had seen Chip pitch in the opening game.

"You were too good for our players," the young man said.

"Fortunate would be more like it," Chip said with a smile.

"How long have you been pitching, Mr. Hilton?" The young woman asked.

"This is my second year in college, but I also pitched two years in high school."

Chip was impressed by the perfect English spoken by Tamio's guests. As the conversation continued, he was further amazed at their knowledge of American sports.

A little later in the evening an older woman, whom Tamio called mama-san, entered. She was carrying a *koto,* a traditional Japanese musical instrument. After bowing nearly to the floor several times, she turned and two girls appeared and also bowed several times. The girls could not have been more than sixteen years old, but they were elegantly dressed in kimonos and obis, and their hair was piled high on top of their heads. They wore jeweled combs and pearls and carried fans.

"They are young geisha girls, *hangyoku*," Tamio whispered. "In training. Geisha means 'accomplished person.'"

The older woman and girls sat at the table and joined in the conversation. After a short time, the woman began to strum the koto. Rising from the table, the girls began a slow, graceful dance, singing in Japanese with a strange, measured, rhythmical harmony that Chip found eerie but melodious.

A little later, when the young couple said it was time for them to leave, Chip got a big thrill. Tamio's guests asked Chip for his autograph. He felt embarrassed, but he signed the card to honor their request.

> *To Tamio's Honorable Friends,*
> *Thank you for a very special*
> *evening in Japan.*
> *William "Chip" Hilton*

Then he got a shock. Tamio pulled the State University autographed No-Hitter game ball out of his pocket and handed it to the young man! "This is an honorable gift from Chip-san," he said, bowing deeply.

The young man smiled happily. "This is a great honor," he said, bowing to Chip and Tamio. "It will be a treasured gift."

Tamio walked back to the hotel with Chip, talking about everything but his guests. Chip had enjoyed seeing the talented geisha girls and thoroughly appreciated the special evening. But he was troubled that Tamio had given away the special baseball, a precious gift of his own, to his guest. Chip said nothing, however, as he didn't know how to approach it. Instead he tried to thank his new friend for the wonderful evening. But, as usual, Tamio shrugged it off.

"It was insignificant, Chip-san. It was my humble privilege, but I must go now. We will practice tomorrow morning, yes?"

"Sure thing, Tamio-san, 9:30."

Chip returned to his room and began surfing through TV channels. Shortly before eleven o'clock, Soapy arrived. As soon as he opened the door, the redhead was bubbling over with tales of his latest adventures. "What an experience!" he cried. "And what a game!"

"Who played?"

"The Yakult Swallows and the Yomiuri Giants. There's a big-league game every night. Man, what a crowd!"

"How many?"

"Over fifty thousand. Get this—the place is called the Big Egg, and the Giants' mascot is a humongous rabbit," Soapy said delightedly.

"Who won?"

"We had to leave before it was over so we'd make curfew, but the Swallows were ahead 7-6 when we left. Man, are those fans loud! They even have special cheering sections, just like the college teams here—only they're bigger and louder!"

"How big's the field?"

"Well, the walls in left and right field are kinda close, I'd say a little over three hundred feet."

"Any home runs?"

"Yeah, sure! Three or four. Hey, Chip, did you know that a Japanese player hit 868 home runs during his career?"

"Yeah, I think his name was 'Sadahara Oh—amazing,' or something like that."

Soapy shrugged his shoulders, knowing Chip was the wrong person to show off his baseball knowledge to. "I know how good some Japanese players are since guys like Hideo Nomo and Hideki Irabu play in our major leagues. But this Oh guy is news to me."

"Here's another one for you, Soapy. Katsuya Nomura, called the 'Johnny Bench of Japan,' hit 657 homers *and* caught 2,918 games."

"Wow! A catcher just like me . . ."

Soapy's mood changed abruptly. He dropped down heavily on a chair by the desk. "You think the Rock's gonna let me play in any of the games?" he asked sadly.

"Sure, Soapy. Just as soon as he thinks your thumb is all right. You know the Rock. He wouldn't bring you all the way over here to sit on the bench. Come on. Let's call it a day. It's after eleven."

Tamio was waiting for Chip and Soapy the next morning, and once more they worked out in the stadium. Afterward, they went for another drive, had a quick lunch at a noodle shop near the Imperial Hotel, and drove to the game in Tamio's car.

Jingu Stadium was jammed. Keio's victory the previous day had brought the fans out in droves. The crowds were hilariously happy and hungry for another win over the Statesmen. The Keio victory had also fired up the Waseda players. They were determined to equal the showing made by their archrivals.

Rockwell started Pete "Repeat" Phillips on the mound and Patrick "Patty" Patterson behind the plate. Both were recruits from the freshman team, and this was their first opportunity to work in a game with the varsity. Chip, Diz Dean, Doogie Dugan, Al Engle, and Soapy loosened up in the bull pen in right field and watched the game.

Repeat Phillips was a short, stocky southpaw. He had an assortment of pitches, but he was nervous and erratic. In the sixth inning, with State leading 3-0, he faltered badly.

He accidentally hit the first batter and walked the second. The third hitter singled to fill the bases. Rockwell called time and motioned for Dean to go in.

"Here I go again," Dean grumbled as he left the bull pen. "I wonder how it would feel to *start* a game—"

"You don't start a game with a three-run lead," Dugan said calmly.

"Nor with the bases loaded!" Dean retorted as he stalked away.

State's three-run lead vanished with Dean's first pitch. To the unrestrained joy of the spectators, the batter laced a grand-slam home run over the right-field wall, putting Waseda ahead 4-3. The Waseda fans erupted with cheers of "*Manrui* homer! *Manrui* homer!"

Dean was effective after that, but so was the Waseda pitcher. With no one down in the bottom of the ninth, Rockwell sent Chip in to hit for Murphy Gillen. Chip responded with a stand-up double. Speed attempted to move Chip over to third with a bunt and instead popped up to the catcher.

Then Patterson struck out for the second out. Red Schwartz, hitting for Diz Dean, drilled a hard liner into the outfield. The Waseda right fielder made a diving catch for it and the third out. Chip died on second as Waseda set the Statesmen down for their second straight loss. It was quiet as they headed off the field, losers for two straight games.

After the players had showered and dressed, Coach Rockwell held a brief meeting in the locker room. "Well, men," he said grimly, "I guess we realize that we're up against two first-class ball clubs. We have no excuses and no complaints. We played hard and tried hard and we were beaten in both games by better teams. However, I do think that this is in part due to being exposed to a lot more excitement than we're accustomed to during the past eleven days.

"Tomorrow is Sunday, and I have called off all sightseeing. I expect everyone to rest up with a quiet day, and I want all of you to be present for our team meals at breakfast, lunch, and dinner in the hotel. They've reserved a small dining room for us. Also, there's a church directory in the lobby for those interested.

"Monday we'll visit Nikko, leaving from the hotel at 9:30 A.M. That's all. Oh, yes, I'd like to suggest, in case you haven't already done so, that each of you take time to write home."

Chip had invited Tamio to church earlier in the week and was delighted when he called Saturday night and said he would come. Chip was pleased as they made plans to meet in the morning. He and Soapy were looking forward to attending church in Japan, and Tamio seemed happy to join them.

After breakfast Sunday morning the two waited outside the hotel lobby for their friend to pick them up. As usual, Tamio was right on time. He greeted them cheerfully as they hopped into his car. Tamio assured them it was only a short drive to the church, smiling as they hunched over to fit comfortably.

The two State players were surprised at the number of Americans present in the congregation. Chip especially appreciated the church's bilingual approach, singing songs in both Japanese and English. The minister, a kind Japanese man who reminded Chip and Soapy of their pastor in Valley Falls, greeted them warmly at the door as they left. In the afternoon they took a long walk with Tamio through several parks adjoining the hotel. They finished up the day by catching up on E-mails in the hotel's business center and watching some TV.

Monday morning, after breakfast, the University Statesmen assembled in front of the hotel and boarded several vans to the train station. Tamio was waiting at the ticket counter, and during the trip to Nikko, he, Chip, Soapy, and Biggie shared a double seat. Soapy had learned about Nikko from some of his Japanese friends and was pleased to expound on his knowledge with a helpful word here and there from Tamio. Biggie and Chip looked on with amusement as Tamio continued to help their pal with his Japanese.

They lunched American-style at the Kanaya Hotel and then visited the Sacred Bridge that crossed the Daiya River. The bridge rested on two great stones shaped to resemble *torii,* or gates. The bridge was red-lacquered and reserved solely for religious assemblies and ceremonies.

Their next stop was at the Toshogu Shrine. This huge structure was the most elaborate shrine in all Japan. They changed from shoes to slippers and walked through a large granite torii. Just inside was a pagoda. Walking upward on the stone steps, they passed the Front Gateway and proceeded on to the Sacred Stable. This building was decorated with wooden carvings of monkeys. Here they found the original carving of the three world-famous monkeys who "hear no evil, speak no evil, see no evil."

After examining the intricate carvings, they continued toward the Sacred Cistern and Sacred Library. This massive structure revolved between a huge belfry and a drum tower. They passed an intricately fashioned gate decorated in gold and white, with hundreds of carvings of children and prophets adorning its surface.

The Inner Court contained three Sacred Portable Shrines, and Tamio explained that these honored Yoritomo Minamoto, Japan's first shogun; Hideyoshi Toyotomi, the great dictator-shogun; and Ieyasu Tokugawa, founder of the Tokugawa Shogunate.

"Ieyasu Tokugawa was a great leader," Tamio said proudly. He waved his arm to take in the buildings and surroundings. "The Toshogu Shrine was made to honor Tokugawa."

There were other buildings in the Inner Court. Tamio described them as the Sacred Dance Stage, the Upper Shrine Office, the Chinese Gate, the Oratory, and the Main Hall.

TAMIO'S HONORABLE FRIENDS

"It is the inner sanctum here," Tamio said. "We are not permitted to enter. Inside is a great shrine for the three deities." He paused a moment and then added, "There are mirrors." Tamio nodded toward the closed door. "The sacred ashes of Ieyasu Tokugawa are there in the mausoleum."

A little later the entire party visited Lake Chuzenji and the Kegon Waterfall. Then they returned to the Kanaya Hotel for dinner. Chip and his pals had been affected deeply by the fabulous shrines and enjoyed an experience they would never forget.

Tamio left them at the station in Tokyo. "I will see everyone tomorrow," he said, "at the game in Sendai. Tamio will watch the game from the illustrious bull pen."

"That goes for me too," Soapy added consolingly. "I'm a catcher, but I watch all the games from the outfield lately."

When the Statesmen arrived back at the Imperial Hotel, it was nearly eleven o'clock. Coach Rockwell sent them to their rooms. "Breakfast is at 7:30 tomorrow morning," he announced. "We leave at nine from the lobby. We're traveling to Sendai by train—the Yamabiko Super Express—and we play Keio in the afternoon. Then we're going on to Sapporo from Sendai to play Waseda on Wednesday. We won't be back here until Friday. Get a good night's rest."

CHAPTER 14

A Third-Strike Bunt

THE YAMABIKO Super Express train from Tokyo to Sendai Tuesday morning took just over ninety minutes. The team registered at the Sendai Hotel, and after a light lunch the players took two vans to the ballpark. Just before they ran out onto the field, Coach Rockwell gave the team a little pep talk.

"We've lost two in a row, but we're rested now. And we're the home team; we have the last bats. Chip will pitch, and if you men can get him a couple of runs, we can even the series with Keio. Now let's go!"

Al Engle and Chip warmed up in front of the State dugout. Across the field, in front of the Keio dugout, the same pitcher who had beat the Statesmen in Tokyo was throwing from the warm-up rubber.

Chip felt rested and right. After the formal pregame ceremonies, which had been part of all their games in Japan, he walked out to the mound to start the game. Chip threw several pitches to Engle, and when the umpire called, "Play ball!" he tucked his glove under his arm and turned to look toward the pitchers in the bull pen. He saw Tamio leaning against the rail and gestured a greeting with the ball. Tamio waved back, and then Chip shifted his gaze toward center field.

Standing there, polishing the game ball in his bare hands, he studied the scoreboard. Keio was in the top spot with State below in the home-team slot. He turned to face Keio University's leadoff hitter and concentrated on Al Engle's sign. From the dugout, he could hear Soapy yelling his encouragement, and behind him, his Statesmen teammates were starting their usual game chatter. He blazed his fastball around the batter's knees.

"Strike!"

Chip got the first batter on three straight pitches. The number-two hitter drove a hard single to right field, and the third Keio batter went down swinging. With the count at three and one, Keio put on the hit and run. The runner took off, but the batter missed Chip's curveball by a foot. Al Engle pegged the ball to Speed Morris, and the runner was out by ten feet.

No runs, one hit, no errors.

The Statesmen went right to work when they came in for their licks in the bottom of the initial inning. Ozzie Crowell singled. Minson's sacrifice bunt advanced Ozzie to second, and Belter Burke doubled to right field, allowing Crowell to score the first run of the game. Biggie lifted a fastball over the right-field wall for a home run and two more runs.

Fireball cut under a fastball, and the catcher gathered in the ball for a second out. Murphy Gillen went down swinging for the third out, but State led at the end of the first inning, 3-0.

In the top of the second inning, Keio's first batter caught one of Chip's fastballs on the nose for a solid triple. The next hitter, batting left-handed, laid a perfect drag bunt down the first-base path, and the man on third beat Biggie's peg to the home plate. The third hitter drove a hard grass cutter directly across third base, and Minson made the difficult stop. Pivoting, he fired the ball to Crowell, who relayed to Cohen for a double play. Chip struck out the next hitter to retire the side with one run, two hits, no errors.

It was a low scoring game, but the Statesmen managed to stay out in front. But in the top of the ninth, leading by the slender margin of 5-3, Chip and the Statesmen ran into trouble.

The Keio leadoff hitter looked at an outside pitch and then squarely met one of Chip's fastballs. The ball flew toward the left-field fence for a clean double. The next batter bunted along the first-base path on the first pitch.

The play was custom-made for Biggie Cohen. He dashed in, scooped up the ball with his left hand, and made a clothesline throw to Minson on third. The veteran third baseman dropped the ball, and the hitter advanced to second base, carrying the tying run. Rockwell called time and walked out to the mound.

Minnie Minson angrily dug his spikes into the ground. "It's my fault," he said in disgust. "Biggie made a perfect peg. I should have had it."

"Never mind," Rockwell called. "Forget it!" He paused beside Chip and looked at the scoreboard. "Too bad, Chip," he said. "It was a tough break."

Al Engle joined them. "They'll probably try a couple of squeeze plays to tie up the score," he said. "There's no one down."

Coach Rockwell grunted and said, "I wouldn't be surprised." Rockwell eyed the Keio batter who was waiting patiently outside the batter's box. He glanced at the scoreboard and, speaking his thoughts aloud, said, "It's against all the principles of good baseball to put the winning run on base, but it will give us a play at any base, and I have a hunch it's the right thing to do."

Rockwell pondered a moment longer and then headed for the dugout. "Put him on, Chip," he said decisively over his shoulder. "Load the bases!"

"Excellent!" Engle declared, thumping his catcher's glove. "We'll get 'em, Coach." He walked back to the plate and crouched to give the sign.

Chip threw four straight pitchouts to Engle, and the umpire waved the hitter to first base.

Bases loaded! No one down! Cleanup hitter at bat!

Engle moved out in front of the plate and tossed the ball to Chip. "No one down, guys," he yelled. "Let's get 'em at any base now!"

The infield moved in, and Chip faced the Keio power hitter. *One thing's for sure,* Chip told himself. *I'm not going to get behind in the count. I'm not walking in any runs!*

The batter dug in and gave the impression that he was going to blast the ball out of the park. Chip took no chances. He fired a low, deceptive screwball that cut sharply back across the outside corner for the first strike. The batter whirled for the bunt but let the ball go when he thought it would be too low. He stepped out of the batter's box.

When the batter stepped back up to the plate, Chip came right back with a low, fast curve that caught the same corner for strike two. The hitter again stepped back out of the box, looking toward the first-base coaching box for guidance.

Chip backed away from the rubber and checked the runners. Then he studied the batter. "He might do it," Chip breathed. "He just might try it."

He glanced over toward Soapy. The redhead was lifting his hands, palms up, toward the dugout roof.

Henry Rockwell had waved the infield back, and Engle squatted to give the sign. When the hitter stepped into the batter's box, Chip toed the rubber and fired a shoulder-high fastball. His follow-through carried him partway down the alley, and he landed in a low crouch with his hands ready for anything.

Almost before the release of the ball, Chip saw the runners take off and the hitter shorten up on his bat. *Right! A third-strike bunt!* he exulted.

The play fooled Rockwell and the Statesmen, but not Chip. The hitter dumped the ball fifteen feet down the alley, and Chip dove headlong for the ball, his right hand outstretched at full length. He grasped the ball and tossed it all in one motion to Engle, who was tagging the plate. The play was close, but the ball beat the runner for the first out.

Right then, Al Engle proved he was a topnotch receiver. Before the umpire's hand flashed in the air, Al had cocked his arm and fired the ball to first base. Biggie had advanced toward the plate with Chip's throw, and Ozzie Crowell was covering first. The ball beat the runner by a stride, and the Statesmen had a double play.

The play had been almost too fast to see. It was major-league baseball, and the crowd's tremendous cheer testified to their appreciation of the State players' lightning reactions and synchronized teamwork.

Ozzie came trotting to the plate with the ball and handed it to Engle. There were two down with runners on second and third.

Chip dusted off his uniform and walked back to the mound. On the way, he checked the scoreboard once more. The score remained the same: State 5, Keio 3. "Two down and one to go," Chip breathed.

The next batter was the Keio first baseman. As he strode to the plate, Engle called time and met Chip in front of the mound. "He hits lefty, Chip," Engle fretted. "And he's had two for three. Let's keep 'em low and try to make him hit it in the dirt."

Chip nodded and waited until Engle was set behind the plate. The runners on second and third danced back and forth, trying to distract him. But Chip concentrated on the plate and took his stretch. Then he let loose with a low, wicked curveball inside for ball one. The stands were in an uproar. He tried his screwball next, and it darted down and away from the hitter, missing the corner for ball two. It was pandemonium now! The Keio and State players and the crowd were yelling at the top of their voices.

Engle called for a low fastball. Chip toed the rubber, and the runners went into their dancing act. Chip focused on the target, Engle's big glove, and started his motion. At the very top of his stretch, he saw Engle's right thumb flicker. It startled him and his heart jumped. But he started down with the ball.

At the last instant he whipped his left leg toward third base and fired the ball for the hot corner. For one wild second he was afraid Minson had missed the sign. Then he saw Minnie dart for the bag and the ball plunked into his glove. The runner was caught; he had tried too late to get back! They had him trapped between third and home.

Chip headed for home to back up Engle, but Biggie was already there. So he continued on behind Biggie. Speed was behind third base, and Belter Burke was behind Speed. But Engle and Minson didn't need any help. Jaime "Minnie" Minson chased the speedy runner a few steps toward the plate and fired the ball to Engle. Engle charged up the base path and threw to Minson. When Minnie got the ball, he faked a return throw to Engle, suddenly turned on the speed, ran the hapless runner down, and tagged him ten feet in front of the plate.

The game was over! The Statesmen had survived the hectic last inning to win by 5-3.

The State players were exuberantly celebrating the victory when Soapy and Tamio joined Chip in front of the dugout. The three friends stood there and watched the crowd. Tamio congratulated Chip and said he was leaving with his teammates. "We fly south to Tokyo now, Chip-san. You fly north to the island of Hokkaido. You will play Waseda tomorrow in Sapporo. Hokkaido is a beautiful, cold country; it has many volcanoes. It still has big farms and many cows and sheep."

"Good food?" Soapy queried with a slight grin.

"Oh, yes. Soapy-san will enjoy his meals." Tamio laughed. "I must go now. We play State again in Jingu Stadium on Friday."

Chip grasped Tamio's arm. "Wait a second, Tamio-san. I've seen your team's top two pitchers now, and I think you're just as good as they are. Honest!"

"Right!" Soapy agreed. "Maybe you'll pitch against us on Friday."

Tamio shrugged his shoulders. "It will never happen. Our number-two pitcher is fine for Friday. However, I am practicing much. Maybe my chance will come." He bowed to Chip and then to Soapy and walked swiftly toward the Keio dugout.

Chip and Soapy watched their protégé until he ducked down into the dugout across the field. Then they started for the State locker room. "It's too bad he doesn't get a chance," Chip said.

"You've got that right," Soapy agreed. "I watched the Keio pitcher last Friday, and I watched the guy today like a hawk. Tamio is as good or even better."

"Unless—" Chip began.

"Unless what?"

"Unless he loses his control under pressure or freezes up in a game."

Soapy shook his head. "I don't think he'd lose his control, Chip. And as for choking, I don't think he would know how. I've never seen a guy so determined to be a pitcher. Hey! I've got an idea! If we make sure we keep beating those two Keio pitchers, Tamio's bound to get a chance."

"If only we could knock them both out of the box in the same game," Chip mused aloud, "that might do it."

"There's got to be a way," Soapy concluded. "Just got to."

CHAPTER 15

"Boys, Be Ambitious"

SOAPY SMITH yawned, stretched, and slid his Walkman into his backpack. Standing up, he reached his strong, freckled hands into the overhead compartment. "Here, Chipper, here's your bag. Hey, Biggie, want me to get yours?" The team filed down the plane's narrow aisle behind Coach Rockwell and then followed him up the jetway into the New Chitose Airport terminal.

At the gate, coaches and players from the University of Hokkaido were waiting to welcome them. Several athletes carried large posters with the words Welcome State University Statesmen elegantly stenciled on them in red and blue ink. "Man, look at that poster! The writing looks like the calligraphy we saw in Tokyo," Speed murmured. "It's really beautiful."

"Yeah, and they used our school colors," Soapy said happily. "That's really a nice touch. Good food and good manners—I may have to move here someday."

Biggie and Speed looked at each other and in unison cried, "Not!" Speed dissolved in laughter and slapped Biggie a high-five. Soapy appeared indignant, but he was welcomed at that moment by several Japanese students who instantly grabbed his attention.

At the baggage carousel, the Statesmen retrieved their own luggage and then helped their Japanese hosts, who had already begun pulling the State University equipment bags. Bags and equipment flew onto metal carts, and within minutes, the two groups were walking to the team bus parked outside at the curb. Chip, Soapy, Biggie, Speed, Red, and Fireball took seats near one another in the back, and they were quickly joined by one of the Hokkaido players.

"My name is Chosei Araki. The Hokkaido team is very excited about your arrival."

As the players talked, they learned that Sapporo was Araki's home and that the city was about twenty-five miles away. Araki was friendly and courteous and told them he was a catcher and loved baseball. "I play for the university," he said proudly.

"How many students are in your school?" Soapy asked.

"We have several thousand," Chosei said, his voice filled with pride. "It is a very good school."

"Is Sapporo big?" Chip asked.

Chosei waved his hand in a big circle. "It is a large city," he answered.

The bus slowed down and pulled to the side of the highway. "We will stop to see the statue of Clark-san," Chosei explained seriously. "He was a great American teacher at our university."

The players lumbered off the bus and grouped in front of a high, granite pillar. A bronze plaque bearing the face of a man and a number of Japanese characters was attached to the surface.

Their host pointed to the plate. "It is a dedication to Clark-san. Note the date of 1871. The writing says: 'Boys, be ambitious.'"

"Why is the statue located here?" Chip asked, looking around.

"That is a good question," Chosei said, "but the explanation is simple. When Clark-san left the university to return to America, his students came with him to this point. Here he made the statement: 'Boys, be ambitious.' Clark-san was a much-honored man."

They piled back into the bus and soon reached the outskirts of the city. Here they found broad, tree-lined boulevards, with each crossing the other at right angles. "What is this?" Soapy exclaimed. "Philadelphia?"

It was late when they checked in at the Sapporo Grand Hotel after more sightseeing. The players sat around in the lobby and talked to their hosts until it was time to go up to their rooms for lights out.

After breakfast the next morning, the team visited the university and found a school that rivaled their own alma mater in facilities, equipment, and distinguished faculty. After an early lunch, they climbed back on the bus to ride to Maruyama Stadium. The Waseda team was already warming up on the field, having flown in from Tokyo that morning.

Before the game, during Waseda's hitting practice, Soapy put on quite a show entertaining the young boys and girls sitting with their parents behind the dugout. First, he wiggled his swollen thumb in the air to get their attention. Then he apparently made it disappear. Next, he did tricks with the ball, flipping it between his legs and behind his back and then rolling it up one arm, behind his neck, and down the other arm.

But the show wasn't only for the kids. Soapy was glancing out of the corner of his eye at Coach Rockwell and cutting loose on his throws to Chip. It was obvious to all his teammates that Soapy was trying to prove that his thumb was all right. "How'd you like that one, Chipper?" he cried, glancing at Rockwell.

Coach Rockwell shook his head and smiled. "A few more days, Soapy," he called, "and then we'll see."

State University was the home team in this game. Coach Rockwell started Diz Dean on the mound and Patrick "Patty" Patterson behind the plate. Then he sent Chip, Repeat, and Doogie to the bull pen with Al and Soapy.

It was a free-hitting and free-scoring game. Waseda bolted into the lead by scoring two runs in the top half of the first inning. State came right back and tied it up in their turn at bat, and that's the way it went. Waseda would score and State would match the pace.

In the sixth inning, Diz became more erratic and couldn't get the Waseda hitters out. Before Rockwell could get Phillips ready to relieve the erratic southpaw, Waseda had scored four runs, the bases were loaded, and there was only one out. Repeat Phillips managed to put out the fire, but Waseda scored one more run to keep a steady lead with a score of 12-6.

State got three of the runs back in the bottom of the same inning, and Phillips handcuffed the opposing hitters through the seventh, eighth, and ninth. When State came in for their last hits, the score was 12-9.

Speed led off and worked the Waseda pitcher for a walk. Patty Patterson had caught a fine game but hadn't touched the ball as a batter. Rockwell called Engle and Chip in from the bull pen. He sent Engle in to pinch hit for the young catcher.

Engle justified Coach Rockwell's confidence by lining a two-bagger to right field, sending Speed to third. Then Rockwell sent Chip in to bat for Phillips. Chip walked up to the plate, representing the tying run.

He had been watching the soft stuff the pitcher relied on, mentally setting himself up to face the possibility of a pinch-hit call from Rockwell. Now he was ready. He took the first pitch, a ball, looked at a strike, and then went for a belt-high inside curveball. He met it with the meat of the bat, pulling it over first base. The ball lit just inside the right-field foul line and rolled to the fence.

Speed and Engle scored, and Chip held up at third. Waseda was now leading 12-11. There was no one down and the tying run was on third base.

"Nice hitting, Chip," Rockwell said. "Heads up now. We've got to tie up the score."

Chip watched every move the pitcher made. He wasn't going to get picked off. He kept one foot on the base until the Waseda pitcher took his stretch. Then he edged away from the bag, leading off in foul territory, ready for anything.

Ozzie Crowell was an ideal leadoff man. He had a good eye and could bunt or hit. He took the first pitch for a ball and then put on the squeeze. The Waseda pitcher evidently anticipated the play because he came in with a shoulder-high fastball.

Chip was away with the pitch, and Ozzie came through with a bunt. But the result was a little roller directly up the alley to the advancing pitcher. The hurler fielded the ball underhand and flipped it to the catcher just as Chip slid for the plate.

The catcher's tag beat Chip to the plate, and the umpire's "Out!" was the right call. But that wasn't the end of the play. Ozzie had turned first and headed for second. Right after tagging Chip, the Waseda receiver fired the ball down to second base. The shortstop tagged Ozzie for the out. Two away!

Minnie Minson was a great batter in the second slot and a strong hitter. He had batted second in the hitting order for two straight years and was an expert in that important position. He walked up to the plate as State's last chance to win the game.

The pitcher fed Minnie his fastball, and the husky third-base guardian lined a hard hit toward second base. The Waseda second baseman made a desperate one-hand stab at the ball and caught it. The game was over. Waseda had beaten the Statesmen two out of the three games they had played. The score: Waseda 12, State 11.

The Statesmen were unusually quiet as they showered and dressed. This was getting serious. To win the six-game series with Waseda they would have to come out on top in the three remaining games. The only bright spot was the fact that they had broken even with Keio so far.

Chosei Araki was waiting outside the locker room when Chip, Soapy, and Biggie appeared. He rushed up to Chip and bowed several times. "I am extremely sorry," he said. "I did not recognize you as Hilton-san. I am honored to meet a great no-hitter pitcher and his friends. I am also pleased to be your escort while your team is in Sapporo. Please follow me to your team bus. Many Japanese fans have read about the no-hitter game Hilton-san pitched in Tokyo."

Chip was pleased but embarrassed. Trying to hide his feelings, he said, "It was a funny game. Every time the Waseda players hit the ball, one of my teammates was in the right spot. Besides, the Waseda hitters weren't ready."

It was a good effort, but it didn't work. The four players walked to the team bus, talking baseball nonstop. Chosei continued to talk about the no-hit game. He evidently had his own ideas about such sterling performances.

After dinner, for the second night in a row, the Statesmen explored a few shopping areas near the hotel, taking in the sights, sounds, and character of Sapporo.

The next day, after their team breakfast, they broke into small groups. Their hosts drove them along the coast to Noboribetsu. On the way they noted the hundreds of inns and hotels. Hot-water pools and baths were everywhere. At noon they lunched Japanese-style at the Dai-ichi Takimoto, a hotel noted for its multitude of pools, each with varying temperatures and mineral contents. It was a wonderful, relaxing day, and it was a happy ball club that returned to the hotel that evening.

Parting with the host was sad. He and the other Hokkaido player-hosts rode with the State University team to the airport early Friday morning and walked the team down the concourse to their gate. Chosei was still waving good-bye as Chip, Soapy, and Biggie turned to give a final thumbs-up to their new friend before disappearing through the jetway entrance. Even with their short stay in Sapporo, the four baseball players had developed a warm friendship.

That afternoon, back in Tokyo, Coach Rockwell started Dugan against Keio. It was another free-hitting contest. The State batters hit Keio's number-one hurler hard in the first two innings to score four runs. But in the third inning, they really poured it on, batting through the order to score five runs and drive the starting pitcher to the showers.

Unfortunately, the Keio hitters were having a field day with Dugan and matched the Statesmen run for run. In the sixth inning they got a big rally going and scored four runs to take the lead by one, 14-13. The bases were loaded when Rockwell lifted Dugan and called on Phillips. The sophomore managed to pull through the inning but was forced to give up one more run. That made the score: Keio 15, State 13.

State scored twice in the seventh to tie up the score at fifteen all, but Keio came right back in the eighth to drive Phillips off the mound and score two runs in the process. The bases were loaded with one down when Dean replaced Phillips. Diz was wild, but a double play by Minson and Crowell pulled the big pitcher out of a tough spot. The Statesmen came in for their last at bat behind by two: Keio 17, State 15.

Rockwell sent Chip in to hit for Dean, and he raised the Statesmen's hopes by parking the second pitch over the right-field wall for a home run. Crowell sent a sizzler toward the hole at short, but the Keio infielder scurried back and fielded the ball. His throw beat Ozzie to the bag by a stride for the first out.

Minson fouled out, and Belter Burke lifted a towering fly to left field that the Keio outfielder easily pulled in for out number three. The score: Keio 17, State 16.

The Statesmen had now lost four of the six games they had played in Japan, and it was clear to Rockwell and the veteran players that State really had only one first-class pitcher—Chip Hilton. Chip had pitched a no-hitter to beat Waseda 1-0, and he had set Keio down, 5-3.

Offensively, the team was doing all right, having scored forty-six runs in six games. And, defensively, only two errors had been committed. It was the pitching. State's pitching weakness was obvious.

Tamio was waiting outside the stadium as usual, and Chip and Soapy congratulated him on the Keio victory.

"Nice win, Tamio-san." Soapy bowed. "I thought for sure they would put you in to pitch in the sixth inning."

Tamio smiled. "It will never happen. Keio can win without me."

"Keio wouldn't have won if Chip had been pitching," Soapy said. "Your top two pitchers are gonna get their ears really pinned back one of these days, and then your manager or coach, or whatever he's called, will have to give you a chance."

"I think not, Soapy-san. However, I practice control when pitching in batting practice. I throw three balls at the catcher's right shoulder, three at his left shoulder, then three at his knees. Now I can put the ball right where I want."

"You ought to vary your targets, too, Tamio," Chip suggested.

Tamio nodded. "It is good advice. I will throw one ball at each target from now on."

Chip and Soapy exchanged a quick glance. Tamio never missed a trick. One thing was for sure; he was going to be ready when his chance came.

"We won't be able to work out tomorrow morning," Chip said. "We play Waseda in Yokohama, and it's my turn to pitch."

"I know," Tamio said. "I will be in Nagoya. I will see you both then. As you say, good luck against Waseda tomorrow."

Chip and Soapy climbed aboard the team bus and headed for the back. As Soapy slumped down into a seat, he expelled a breath of air and shook his head. "It doesn't look very good for next year," Soapy said gloomily.

"Never mind next year," Chip said quickly, sitting down next to his friend. "Let's think about the present. We're not even going to make the series playoffs the way we're going."

"That's for sure," Soapy added. "Anyway, we've got one excuse."

"What's that?"

"Well, they take turns playing us, and that means they always have their best pitchers ready for us."

"That sounds pretty lame to me."

"I didn't mean it that way, Chip. You know, I never realized until today just how important Hex Rickard was—"

"He was great," Chip interrupted. "We would never have won the conference without him."

"What in the world is Rock going to do for pitchers?"

"Maybe Diz will get over his wildness by next year," Chip said hopefully. "You never know. Maybe Dugan and Phillips will develop on this trip too," he added encouragingly.

CHAPTER 16

"That's Why You Gave Him the Ball!"

THE WASEDA HITTERS had battered State's two lefties, Dean and Phillips, for nineteen hits and twelve runs the previous Wednesday in Sapporo. And they were full of confidence Saturday afternoon when Chip took the mound to fire the first pitch to them in Yokohama.

Chip was feeling great! His pitching motions were fluid, and he felt ready to play a solid game. He set his strong jaw in determination. His fast one was hopping, and when the ball smacked into Al Engle's big glove, the sound echoed like a firecracker.

The Waseda hitters didn't have a chance. Chip was never in trouble and pitched a shutout game—limiting the opposing hitters to three scattered hits—and chalking up fourteen strikeouts.

The Waseda starting pitcher, however, was in trouble from the very first pitch. Crowell and Minson singled, and then Belter Burke cleared the bases with a home run. Biggie followed his lead, and it was 4-0 with no one down when the number-two pitcher walked slowly in from the Waseda bull pen.

Pitcher number two faced the same treatment but with less disastrous results. Fireball doubled and Gillen walked. On the hit-and-run play, Speed drilled a hard ground ball to the first baseman. The double-play ball beat Gillen to second and the return throw to first nipped Speed. Engle struck out to end the inning.

The Statesmen scored two more in the fourth and shelled the number-two pitcher from the mound in the sixth with five runs. Waseda used three more pitchers before the game was over. The final score: State 15, Waseda 0.

It was Chip's third-straight win, and it tied the Waseda series at two games each. The victory gave the Statesmen a big lift, and they were ready to celebrate when they arrived at the New Grand Hotel that evening for dinner.

They arrived in Osaka early Sunday morning and registered at the Osaka Grand Hotel. It was a beautiful hotel. With their early arrival, the players gratefully squeezed in a nap. Later, at the team brunch, Rockwell told them a trip had been arranged to Nara that afternoon; then they would attend a musical revue by the world-famous Takarazuka dancers before continuing on to Nagoya. "We'll have the same rooms when we return from Nagoya," he concluded.

Nara provided many wonderful sights, including a marvelous park. But the three thousand stone lanterns captured the Statesmen's attention. The guide told them that all were lighted during February and August of each year.

That night the team enjoyed a musical and dance revue in Takarazuka. More than three hundred expertly trained performers presented the revue, and the precision and grace with which they performed the intricate dances held the players spellbound. Tamio had told Chip about the years of training the dancers spent in qualifying for their jobs; there was no question about the level of dedication such a career required. After the performance, a team bus drove them back to the Kanko Hotel in Nagoya, and all the players gratefully headed for their beds.

Chunichi Stadium was nearly filled with fans the next afternoon when State took their batting practice. And by the time Keio University had finished hitting, every seat was filled. Chip and Soapy sat in the State dugout and watched Tamio closely as he threw to the Keio hitters during batting practice.

"He wasn't kidding about practicing his control," Soapy said. "He never fails. He throws consistently at each target. And he puts the ball where he wants it every time."

"I know," Chip murmured thoughtfully.

When Tamio threw the last ball, he waved toward Chip and Soapy and walked slowly out to the Keio bull pen. The two pals watched him all the way to the right-field corner.

"You know something, Soapy?" Chip said reflectively. "I think Tamio is a natural."

"Why?"

"Well, for one thing, he has a powerful arm. He can throw every day for batting practice—and he throws hard. In baseball season he throws every day for batting practice. And he's the only one who does it. It's a part of his training."

"That's some system!" Soapy said shortly.

The State hitters were still enjoying their hitting spree. They took up right where they had left off against Waseda, garnering nineteen hits and fourteen runs from the two Keio pitchers. Out in the State bull pen, Chip and Soapy found it hard to understand why the Keio manager let his two best pitchers take such a beating. It was a perfect spot for a young hurler to gain experience.

Diz Dean had a wonderful game with a newfound measure of control. And he went all the way, allowing Keio only four scattered hits. The final score: State 14, Keio 0.

The Statesmen were in a happy, joking mood on the trip back to Osaka. The last two wins had evened up their series with Keio and Waseda. "Now," Soapy proclaimed jubilantly, standing in the aisle, "we're back on the beam and back in the groove. The force is with us!"

But the game of baseball is a game of ups and downs. One day a pitcher has all his stuff and perfect control and can thread a needle with the ball. The next day he can't find the plate. One day a hitter can knock anything and everything out of the park, but the next day he can't hit a ball the size of his hat.

A famous major-league slugger hits successfully fifty or sixty consecutive times at bat and then goes into a slump and can't get a hit to save his life. It's the same with a team. One batter hits safely, another follows suit, then another, and another, and "everybody hits!" And, not infrequently, one or two good hitters will get off to a bad start early in a game and before anyone can say, "Strike!" the rest of their teammates run facefirst into a batting slump.

That's exactly what happened to the Statesmen the next afternoon against Waseda. Rockwell started Dugan, and Doogie pitched a fine game. But this time the State bats were full of holes, and the Nambu Stadium fans went wild as Waseda edged out the Statesmen 5-4.

The defeat set the Statesmen back on their heels again. It was noticeable in the way they left the field and showered and dressed. The locker room was deadly quiet. Coach Rockwell was quick to mark the absence of the usual good-natured teasing, laughter, taunts, and shouts, and when the players finished dressing, he assembled them on the benches.

"It was a tough one to lose, and I know just how you feel. However, someone has to win and someone has to lose. Today we were it. The next time we'll try to see that it's the other guy's turn.

"Tomorrow morning we're leaving at ten o'clock for Kobe. Breakfast is at nine. There's nothing scheduled until Thursday when we play in Hiroshima."

Rockwell paused a moment and then continued. "We'll stop over in Kobe tomorrow night and leave for Hiroshima by train Thursday morning. Now let's relax and forget baseball."

It was raining hard on Thursday morning when the Statesmen's train pulled into Hiroshima. Tamio paced up and down the walk, and as soon as Chip's feet hit the platform, he quickly bowed and then shook Chip's outstretched hand. "I understand the team stays at the New Hiroshima Hotel. Is this right?"

"It sure is, Tamio-san."

"Great, Chip-san. It is raining and now there is no game." Tamio nodded in Henry Rockwell's direction. "Please ask Coach Rockwell if Chip and Soapy-san can visit my home and the home of Frank Okada with me."

Rockwell readily gave his permission, stipulating only that Chip and Soapy return to the hotel for dinner by seven o'clock. Chip and Soapy took the bus with the rest of the team, checked into their room on the tenth floor, and quickly changed clothes. Then they joined Tamio in the lobby.

"We will go to the humble Saito home for lunch." Tamio smiled. "Later, we will visit the home of Frank Okada for tea. Is this all right?"

Chip nodded. "It sounds great, Tamio."

Tamio drove swiftly and surely through the business section of the city and then cut along a broad highway. After a few miles, he turned onto a boulevard and soon reached a neighborhood of small estates. Each house was surrounded by a high fence and was set back from the street. He drove through an open gate and stopped beside a large house with a long, wide porch.

Neatly lined up beside the door, on the traditional Japanese stepping-stone, were several pairs of slippers. Tamio removed his shoes and put on a pair, and Chip and Soapy quickly did the same. Inside the door, a lady and a young girl met them. They bowed several times and then Tamio said, "Chip-san, Soapy-san, please meet my mother and sister, Kinuko."

Tamio's mother led the way along the long hall. The floor was richly polished, and the only sound was the slip-slap of their slippers. Halfway down the hall, Chip saw a large room with sliding walls that were open on three sides of the house.

In the back was a veranda and, beyond this, a garden with walks leading from one section to another. A fountain and small pond dominated the center of the garden. Here, following Tamio's example, they removed their slippers and entered the tatami-covered room in stocking feet.

A gentleman rose from a zabuton beside the low, brown-lacquered table. He was taller than Tamio, but his resemblance to his son was striking. He wore a black silk kimono with red brocade in front. On each sleeve there was a seal also brocaded in red. Tamio's father was partly bald, and his face was smooth shaven. Chip noticed he had Tamio's friendly dark-brown eyes and quick smile.

Bowing to Chip and Soapy, he gestured toward the zabutons beside the table. "Please sit down. I am very honored to meet the friends of my son in our humble home."

Chip and Soapy bowed and sat down on the cushions. Then Mrs. Saito and Kinuko sat down and a maid appeared with green tea.

Chip enjoyed Tamio's family. He learned that Mr. Saito was in the diplomatic service and had once represented Japan in the United States. Chip did not learn in what capacity he had served, but he surmised that Mr. Saito was a man of importance in his country. Tamio's father maneuvered the conversation from baseball to education and finally to their impressions of the customs of the country.

Later, in the same room and at the same large table, two maids served lunch from a sort of tray that Tamio explained was an *ozen*. There were so many courses that even Soapy had to admit defeat! First, there were appetizers of small pieces of roasted chicken, barbecued chicken livers, and ground chicken meat mixed with onion. A main course followed, consisting of barbecued duck and all sorts of vegetables and salads served in small side dishes.

Delicious melon and ices topped it off, followed by tea and cookies so light that Chip could hardly feel them in his hand. He had difficulty with the chopsticks, but Soapy used them expertly, glancing smugly at Chip as he ate.

There was little conversation during the meal. After the tea and cookies, Mr. Saito rose from the table, bowed to Chip and Soapy, and left the room. Mrs. Saito and Kinuko followed, and then Tamio led Chip and Soapy out to the veranda. Here, Chip and Soapy found their shoes waiting.

"The maid brings them," Tamio said as he changed to his shoes. Then he led them down a short flight of steps to the garden. The rain had stopped, and they walked along the stone terraces adjoining the garden.

"Where are the flowers?" Soapy asked curiously.

"There are no flowers in Japanese gardens, Soapy-san, only trees."

"What is Hiroshima noted for?" Chip asked.

"It was an important military city before the catastrophe of the first atomic bomb in World War II," Tamio replied gently. "Now it is known as the Peace City of Japan. There are many peace memorials, houses, bridges, towers, churches, and shrines."

There was a brief silence, and then Tamio glanced at his watch. "There is an important show on television at three o'clock. It is in five minutes. Would you like to see it?"

Chip nodded and followed Tamio and Soapy back up the steps, past the room in which they had eaten lunch, and down the hall to an even larger room. Here they again slipped out of their shoes at the entrance. Sitting down on zabutons, they faced the TV, which was located in a small alcove. As soon as his guests were seated, Tamio closed the sliding walls and turned on the wide-screen TV.

A street scene and festive parade filled the screen. The announcer spoke in Japanese in a high-pitched, almost falsetto voice, evidently describing the parade.

"This is live; it happens now," Tamio clarified.

"THAT'S WHY YOU GAVE HIM THE BALL!"

The camera focused on a long, sleek limousine and then zoomed in on the faces of the car's two occupants. Although Chip had been looking at the scene on TV, he had been thinking about Tamio's family and their hospitality. Suddenly, something on the screen registered. Chip leaned forward for a closer look.

"It's them!" he pointed excitedly. "It's them, Tamio! It's your friends, the guests you entertained in Tokyo."

"It is the crown prince and princess," Tamio said simply.

Chip's jaw dropped. "You mean—"

Tamio nodded. "Yes, Chip-san. They are the next emperor and empress of Japan."

"And the ball! *That's* why you gave him the ball!"

"That is correct, Chip-san. The crown prince has honorable no-hitter ball."

Chip sank back on the zabuton, utterly flabbergasted. He hadn't given the little tea party much thought. Never in his wildest dreams would he have imagined that the crown prince and princess of Japan would meet him informally for tea.

The Stepping-stones

SOAPY SPUTTERED, "You mean the Japanese crown prince got Chip's no-hitter ball?" he asked. Without waiting for an answer, he nodded his head in amazement. "Wow! Well, whaddaya know!"

"That's why there was no one else at the restaurant that night," Chip said thoughtfully.

"That is right, Chip-san. All of the restaurant was reserved that night for the crown prince."

"Whose idea was it?" Soapy asked. "Whose idea was it to get together like that?"

"It was the crown prince, Soapy-san. They saw Chip-san pitch that no-hitter game against Waseda. The meeting was arranged for the crown prince through the Japanese Imperial Household Agency and the director of the tour. The director asked me to be present with Chip-san."

Soapy was absorbed in every word. "What kind of person is he? Does he like sports?"

"Oh, yes, they like all sports. They are now a big part of our people—especially the young people of Japan." Tamio continued slowly, choosing his words carefully. "Many things in Japan are changing all the time. In history, the emperor and his family always lived a very secluded life. People never saw them except in pictures."

Soapy was astonished. "You mean the emperor never rode in parades or made speeches?"

"No, it never happened in our country's past," Tamio explained. "Before World War II, people never even *saw* the emperor. The emperor was a divinity."

"Didn't he ever do any traveling?" Soapy asked.

"When the emperor traveled," Tamio said, "the people knew the emperor was coming and would turn their backs to show reverence. There are many changes in Japan since the old days."

Tamio turned to face Chip. "The crown prince and princess are now part of the people, part of the lives of young persons in Japan. Tamio wishes for Chip-san to understand the new way of life in Japan. The autographed baseball was most precious to me, but for Chip-san to meet and talk with the crown prince and princess and to give the ball to the crown prince means much more. . . . It means a token of the new way and the making of a new tradition." Tamio paused and directly met Chip's glance. "Do you understand?"

While Tamio had talked, Chip had been trying to grasp the greater aspects of the new way of life in Japan. World War II and technological advancements had created many changes.

Women were increasingly finding a place in the political, cultural, and educational life of Japan. Chip remembered the plane they had taken from Tokyo to Sapporo and its logo: "Wings of the New Japan." Although much of traditional Japan remained, international companies resided in Japan and Japanese technology was now globally acclaimed. The large department stores and clothing and stadiums all testified to the changes.

And, as Tamio was trying to explain, the tradition of divinity that had once been associated with the emperor was now a part of history. The future emperor and empress enjoyed closer contact with the joys and sorrows of the people. "It's too big for me to fully understand," Chip told himself.

He looked at Tamio at last and nodded. "I understand part of the great change, Tamio-san. And I am very happy that you made it possible for me to meet the crown prince and princess. They were very gracious."

"You do not mind about the ball?"

"Of course not, Tamio-san. I am greatly honored that the crown prince would accept it as a souvenir."

"It is more than a souvenir," Tamio said fervently. "It is more like a symbol."

Chip glanced at his watch; the time had gotten away from them. "It's nearly four o'clock—"

Tamio smiled and nodded. "Yes, that's right. We are expected at the Okada residence at four o'clock. It is a short walk. We will go now."

Their shoes were waiting on the stepping-stone. Only a little while ago they had removed them on the veranda.

"Someone around here can read your mind, Tamio-san," Soapy said with a chuckle. "I could get used to this!"

"They are fine persons," Tamio agreed, smiling.

It was only a little way to the Okada home. A maid met them at the door, and they changed quickly into slippers on the stepping-stone. They were escorted through a long hall and into a room lined with books. A tall gentleman dressed in a gray business suit rose from the low chair in which he had been sitting, and a lady dressed in a kimono and obi rose quickly from a zabuton beside the table.

The gentleman laid aside a thick book and smiled a welcome to Tamio. Then he faced Chip and Soapy and bowed graciously. "You are Chip Hilton," he said in perfect English.

"We are very honored to meet one of Frank's friends. This is Mrs. Okada."

Chip bowed and smiled, then introduced Soapy. Their host shook hands with each of them and gestured toward the zabutons surrounding the table. "Please be seated," he said.

After Chip and Soapy had arranged their legs the way Tamio had shown Chip before, Mr. Okada clapped his hands softly and a maid entered with tea. While she was serving the tea, Chip studied Mr. and Mrs. Okada. Frank's father was tall, slender, and partly bald. His mustache was sprinkled with wiry gray hairs. Mrs. Okada was small and petite. Her black hair was arranged on top of her head, and her dark-brown eyes were warm and friendly.

Mr. Okada sampled the tea and smiled as he studied his three visitors. "We have been following the games in the papers," he said, smiling at Chip. "You are to be congratulated."

"I've been fortunate," Chip said.

Mr. Okada smiled. "My son Frank has written much about you, and I know exactly how much good fortune and how much true worth are involved in your pitching. By the way, Mr. Smith, I have also heard of your prowess and know of your current injury. I hope you will soon recover."

Mr. Okada then turned to Tamio. "Tamio-san, I have been hoping to see your name in the paper. I trust the opportunity will come soon."

"It will," Soapy said stoutly. "Tamio-san's a fine pitcher."

"Tamio is very ambitious, and I know how much he loves baseball," Mr. Okada said gently. "How is my son Frank, Mr. Hilton?"

Chip told him how well Frank looked and how hard he was studying. "He gets a big kick out of baseball, too, Mr. Okada."

Mr. Okada smiled and nodded. "I know. He wrote me that you had helped him celebrate his birthday. Mrs. Okada and I want to thank you for your kindness to our son."

Mrs. Okada nodded and smiled her thanks. Mr. Okada did most of the talking, and she seemed content to listen. Mr. Okada asked about State. "I am sure Frank told you that State is my alma mater."

Chip and Soapy collaborated in describing State's new buildings, courses, and general progress. It was nearly seven o'clock when they left their friendly hosts. They promised to visit again when State returned for the second game with Hiroshima University.

Tamio drove them to the hotel and promised to be back in an hour. "There is a Carp game tonight," he said pointedly.

"Excellent! Let's go!" Soapy enthused.

"All right," Chip agreed, remembering Tamio's ambition to play for the Carp professional team. "I'd love to see the game."

Tamio was back in an hour, and Chip and Soapy were ready. The glow of the field lights grew stronger as they approached the Hiroshima Citizens' Ball Place. Tamio parked near the stadium and pointed to a high, ghostlike structure. Silhouetted against the reflected glow of the city, Chip could see the gaunt, naked outline of a steel and concrete dome.

"That is where the catastrophe occurred," Tamio said quietly. "The World War II bomb fell on Promotion Hall. This dome and building remain as a memorial."

The bright lights of the surrounding buildings and streets added to the incongruous appearance of the empty spaces of this shattered edifice.

Chip's spirits sank, leaving him with a heavy heart. He wanted desperately to say something, but there just weren't any words to express his feelings. He had read about the almost unbelievable destruction caused by the bomb and been shocked by the tragedy.

"A peace festival is celebrated in Hiroshima every year on August 6," Tamio said. "The Japanese people still worship here on that day."

They continued on to the game, saddened by the brief interlude. At the admission gate a long line of fans was waiting for tickets. The three friends joined in at the end of the line. To Chip, the huge stadium resembled a big bowl cut in half, with the grandstand seats rising, row upon row, behind home plate. Low bleacher sections extended around the outfield.

The incredible enthusiasm of the Carp supporters surprised Chip. They were real fans, cheering and rooting for their favorite players and applauding the plays. The game was definitely big league and very good, but Chip's spirit remained heavy throughout the game. They left in the seventh inning, but they barely made it back to the hotel before eleven o'clock.

"I must see my senpai tomorrow morning," Tamio offered when he stopped in front of the hotel. "He would be honored to meet Chip-san and Soapy-san. Will you come?"

"Sure!" Soapy said impulsively.

Chip thought about it for a second. He hadn't counted on this at all. "Aren't you looking for trouble, Tamio-san?" he asked gently.

"Oh, no, Chip-san," Tamio said quickly. "My senpai always sees me when I come home."

"But what about us? What if he finds out we've been helping you with your pitching?"

Tamio shrugged. "This is a risk Tamio must take."

Chip didn't like it, but he couldn't resist the plea in Tamio's eyes. "All right," he breathed reluctantly. "What time?"

"I will be here at 8:30," Tamio replied happily. "We have lots of time tomorrow before the game."

The sun was warm and bright Friday morning, and Chip and Soapy were up even before the alarm buzzed. After breakfast they headed for the front of the hotel to wait for Tamio. In a few minutes he came along and they were on their way. Tamio was in fine spirits, and during the drive he told them about his senpai.

"He is a fine man and has a good education. He was a great player at Keio."

"What's his name?" Soapy asked.

"It is Yoshiro Fujita, Soapy-san. We are here now."

Tamio pulled up and parked in front of a house that was partly hidden by a high wooden fence. They walked through the gate and along a walk that led to a small porch. Tamio pressed a small button on the door casing, and they heard the soft tinkling of bells inside the house. A maid appeared and bowed, and she and Tamio exchanged a few words in Japanese.

"Mr. Fujita is expecting us," Tamio said, stooping to pull on a pair of slippers. Chip and Soapy struggled into their slippers and followed the maid through the house to a back veranda.

Mr. Fujita was sitting on a zabuton with his back to the wall of the house. He rose to his feet as soon as they appeared. "Welcome to my humble home," he said pleasantly.

Tamio introduced Chip and Soapy to Mr. Fujita, and Chip quickly appraised their host. He was tall, his shoulders were broad, and he carried himself like an athlete. Chip judged he was in his early fifties, but his black hair, unwrinkled face, and sharp brown eyes gave the impression that he was a much younger man.

Mr. Fujita gestured toward the zabutons. "Please sit down. How do you like our baseball teams?"

"They are excellent, Mr. Fujita," Chip said. He gestured toward Soapy. "Mr. Smith is a catcher, but his thumb has been injured. We played in high school together too."

Mr. Fujita turned to Soapy. "How do you like Keio's pitchers?"

Soapy nodded. "Very much. They have fine control."

Mr. Fujita was pleased. "A good friend of mine teaches them," he said.

Soapy was straining at the leash, anxious to put in a good word for Tamio. He leaned forward and cleared his throat. Before Chip could head him off, Soapy was on his way. "Tamio-san is just as good as they are," he said eagerly. "I've watched them pitch for Keio in the games, and I've watched Tamio pitch for the Keio batting practices and I know—"

Soapy paused to get his breath and continued. "A catcher knows more about the pitcher than the pitcher knows about himself. Tamio's got speed and control and a wicked curve-ball. He ought to be a starting pitcher, not a batting practice thrower."

There was a heavy silence, and Soapy suddenly realized he had spoken out of turn. But, as always, the redhead found a way out. "You've done a wonderful job with Tamio, Mr. Fujita. He's got everything! Everything a first-class pitcher needs. I'll bet if you were running the Keio team, Tamio would be pitching!"

Mr. Fujita's expression did not change and it was impossible for Soapy to tell whether he was pleased. He studied Soapy for a long moment. Then he turned and eyed Tamio. "I have not seen Tamio pitch for a considerable time—"

CHAPTER 18

Japan's National Game

TAMIO SAITO was quick to seize the opportunity. He bowed to Mr. Fujita and said, "I have gloves and a ball in my car, honorable Fujita-san. I can get them at once."

Soapy was honest in his words and deliberate in his actions. Before Mr. Fujita could reply, the redhead leapt to his feet. "I'll go with you, Tamio-san. I can catch for you."

Mr. Fujita said nothing as Tamio rose uncertainly to his feet and followed Soapy. Chip wanted to keep the conversation moving and asked his host how baseball had gotten its start in Japan.

It was clear to Chip that baseball was a popular topic with Mr. Fujita. The older man reflected a moment and then spoke surely and authoritatively. "Baseball was brought to Japan in 1873 by two American missionaries, Wilson and Maget, who taught the game to students of the Kaisei School. The Kaisei School is now Tokyo University."

"Baseball is considered America's national pastime," Chip commented. "How about in Japan?"

Mr. Fujita smiled and nodded enthusiastically. "It is the same here. Baseball is considered a national game. All games are sellouts, as you Americans say."

"How about professional baseball?"

"It is big business in Japan," Mr. Fujita said proudly. "The Carp are Hiroshima's team; they are very popular. We have big crowds at all games and all games are televised."

"Will today's game be on TV?"

Mr. Fujita nodded. "It will be televised."

Soapy and Tamio returned then, and Mr. Fujita led the way through the garden to a place where a pitching rubber and plate were located. Tamio was familiar with the spot in the garden and moved without hesitation to the rubber. While he warmed up, Chip and Mr. Fujita continued their conversation. But Chip noticed his host was watching his protégé closely.

After he felt right, Tamio began to cut loose with his fastball. As soon as he saw that Tamio was really burning them in, Mr. Fujita moved over behind him.

Chip grinned to himself and followed. He was thinking back to the first time he had seen Tamio throw. He compared Tamio's use of his shoulder and back and his current speed and control with his original style of pitching. The improvement was almost unbelievable.

Then Tamio began to vary his grip on the ball. The hop on his fastball and sharp-breaking curves was beautiful to watch. Mr. Fujita's expression did not change, but Chip noticed that he moved closer behind his kohai when Tamio threw a change-up with the same motion he used for his fastball. And Chip was positive that Mr. Fujita's eyes widened in surprise when Tamio threw a knuckleball.

"It is enough," Mr. Fujita said at last. "Tamio will be a fine pitcher someday."

"*Someday!*" Soapy exploded incredulously. "He's a fine pitcher right *now!*"

NO-HITTER

There was a brief, heavy silence, and Soapy caught Chip's warning glance immediately. "Yes, sir!" Soapy said respectfully, changing his tone. "He's great and he owes it all to you. To *your* coaching!"

"That's right," Chip echoed. "Tamio owes you a lot, Mr. Fujita."

Mr. Fujita bowed and smiled for the first time. "Thank you, honored guests. I am very happy Tamio has such fine friends. I sincerely hope you honored guests will be friends of Yoshiro Fujita."

A little later, after they had enjoyed a cup of tea, Mr. Fujita shook hands with his guests and they started back to the hotel.

"Well," Soapy said hesitantly, "how do you think we made out with Mr. F?"

"Mr. F?" Tamio repeated blankly.

"He means Mr. Fujita," Chip explained. He nodded toward Soapy. "I think we made out all right, Soapy. What do you think, Tamio-san?"

Tamio grinned. "Mr. F was pleased. I am very happy."

That afternoon in the Hiroshima Citizens' Ball Place, Rockwell selected Chip to pitch against Hiroshima University. While he warmed up in front of the dugout, he located Tamio in the grandstand directly behind home plate. Up above the grandstand, inside the press box, the red eyes of the video cameras and TV cameras focused on the field, and Chip knew that Soapy's Mr. F. was watching the game.

The Statesmen got Chip two runs right off the bat, in the top of the first inning. The margin was all Chip needed, but State scored four more runs before the game ended. Chip pitched carefully, and his teammates gave him steady, errorless support throughout the game. Hiroshima scored a run in the fifth inning, but that was the only time they could get a man beyond first base. The final score: State 6, Hiroshima 1.

Tamio was waiting for Chip and Soapy in the lobby of their hotel after the game. He was bubbling over about Chip's pitching. "I learned much today, Chip-san. I watched you pitch every time. Chip-san never makes a mistake. I had the best seat in the grandstand. I was right behind the catcher."

"I saw you," Chip said, smiling.

"How could you learn anything about pitching in the grandstand?" Soapy demanded.

"It is easy." Tamio smiled. "I make a guess before Chip pitches to the batter."

"A guess?"

"Yes, Soapy-san. I try and guess what kind of pitch Chip-san will throw. Then I watch what happens. Most of the time, I guessed the same. I will remember this."

As the boys got off the elevator on Chip and Soapy's floor, Tamio told them he would not be able to join them in Nagasaki the next day. "I will fly with my team to Nagasaki tomorrow morning," he said sadly, "and I must leave right after that game for Tokyo."

"You mean you won't be in Hiroshima next Wednesday when we play Hiroshima?" Soapy asked.

"No, Soapy-san. I must practice in Tokyo with the team. Keio and State each have two wins now. The Keio players will practice much now to win the series. Tamio *must* pitch every day for batting practice."

"But I thought—" Soapy began.

"Hold it, Soapy," Chip interrupted. "Tamio has to be with his team."

"It is right," Tamio said. "Please don't forget your promise to my honorable parents and to Mr. and Mrs. Okada. Please visit their homes when you return to Hiroshima." Tamio fished a piece of paper out of his pocket. "Here are the addresses. Just show them to the taxi driver."

"We won't forget, Tamio," Chip assured him.

After dinner the Statesmen checked out of the hotel and took the overnight boat to Beppu. It was a pleasant, beautiful night. The happy teammates made a circle of the chairs on the top deck of the boat and sang and talked and joked until it was time to go to bed. It was one of the nicest evenings of the trip for them.

They arrived in Beppu early the next morning and took a bus to Nagasaki. There they registered at the Nishikyushu-daiichi Hotel, which was completely international. After brunch they climbed into the team bus to travel to the baseball park, where Rockwell put them through a long hitting drill.

The extra batting practice seemed to pay off because the State hitters blasted the two Keio top pitchers for twenty-four hits and eighteen runs that night. Diz started the game for State and went for six innings before he got into trouble. Repeat stepped in and finished the game. Keio scored three runs while Dean was on the mound and only two against Phillips. The final score: State 18, Keio 5.

The victory relieved a lot of the team tension that had gripped the players after their 5-4 loss to Waseda the previous Tuesday. Rockwell smiled at the happy shouts, good-natured taunts, and laughter echoing in the locker room. The happy mood carried through the evening and all day Sunday.

Coach Rockwell and most of the team attended church services Sunday morning, and then Chip and his Valley Falls friends took taxis to the top of Mount Inasa to enjoy the view of the great harbor. Later they visited the International Cultural Center and the colossal Peace Statue.

After dinner Coach Rockwell took the team for a long walk and then sent them to bed early.

When Chip and Soapy reached their room, the redhead groaned and flopped down on the bed. "I'm beat," he said wearily, "and I haven't done a thing."

"Who has?" Chip asked.

"Everybody but me! Rock said he was going to let me play over a week ago. I wonder what he's waiting for? Heck, my thumb is all right!"

"There's three more games before the series—" Chip began.

"We won't make the series unless we win Monday," Soapy interrupted.

"Why?"

"Because Waseda has beaten us three out of five times." Soapy spread his hands expressively. "If they win another one—"

"We'll still have a chance."

"How do you figure that?" Soapy queried, sitting up on the side of his bed and pulling off his socks.

"Because we've beaten Keio three out of five."

Soapy nodded. "That's right! I forgot about Keio. All we have to do is beat them once more and they'll be out of luck."

"Tamio too."

"Yeah," Soapy said thoughtfully. He pondered a moment, squeezing toothpaste on his brush. "Hey!" he exploded. "What if we tie up the Waseda series and Keio does the same with us?"

"Then it would be a three-way tie."

"Sure! But what happens then? There won't be time to play the odd games—there won't be time to play the championship series. We play Keio on the fourth, and we leave for home on the seventh."

"There would have to be a sudden-death series on Friday and Saturday," Chip said slowly. "One team would get a bye and play the winner of the first round game for the championship."

"Sudden death is right," Soapy said.

"It's no different from this year's NCAA," Chip replied.

"Except that there were more teams," Soapy added. "Well, *oh-YAH-su-mi nah-sai.*"

"I know," Chip said cheerfully, snapping off the light. "Sleep well yourself."

Chip was dozing off to sleep when he heard Soapy's whisper. "Chip? You asleep?"

"No, Soapy."

"You think Rock will use you tomorrow against Waseda?"

"I don't know, Soapy. Why?"

"Well, you pitched Friday, and you know how he is about giving a pitcher three days' rest."

"It's Dugan's turn."

"Doogie isn't going to beat Waseda, Chip. If you don't pitch, we're going to lose."

"Coach is the boss, Soapy."

"Well, if you pitch, I hope he lets me do the catching."

The wistfulness in Soapy's voice hurt Chip. He couldn't think of anything to say, but he made up his mind right then to speak to Coach Rockwell. Soapy hadn't caught a single inning in Japan and his thumb was fine. Chip knew his best pal's heart was set on playing. One thing was sure. There wasn't anyone in the whole world Chip would rather have for a battery mate. He didn't know much about mental telepathy, but when Soapy was behind the plate and he was pitching, it seemed as if they didn't even need the signs.

Coach Henry Rockwell never failed to marvel at the resilience of Chip Hilton's throwing arm. Now, before the vital game with Waseda in Fukuoka, he leaned against the dugout and watched the tall, blond hurler drill the ball to Soapy Smith. Rockwell's eyes shifted to Soapy at the sound of his bantering.

"Attaboy, Chipper! Let me have 'er baby!" He glanced back toward Chip. The few words his star pitcher had managed to speak to him in confidence about Soapy had verified his own impression about the redhead's thumb.

Rockwell smiled and glanced once more at Soapy. The fun-loving catcher was due for a surprise. He turned to watch Doogie Dugan. The little pitcher was throwing to his favorite battery mate, Al Engle. Beside them, Pete "Repeat" Phillips, the lefty up from the freshman team, was pitching to another sophomore, Pat Patterson. Pete Phillips showed promise as a pitcher, and Patterson had everything a good catcher needed except experience.

A bell clanged. Glancing at his watch, Rockwell walked slowly out to the plate with his fungo bat. Al Engle, Biggie Cohen, Speed Morris, Ozzie Crowell, and Minnie Minson were whipping the ball around the horn, and Diz Dean was lifting high fungo flies to the outfield.

Ten minutes later, when their practice time was up, Rockwell made an unusual move. He waited until the Statesmen trotted in from the field and then asked them to crowd down into the dugout.

"Men," he said, as soon as they quieted, "this is a decisive game. Waseda has beaten us three of the five games we have played against them, and unless we win this afternoon, we could very well be eliminated from the play-off series."

Rockwell paused a short moment and then continued. "All of you are familiar with my favorite axiom: *If you don't play to win, why keep the score?* Well, because I believe so much in that little slogan, I'm pleased a number of you came to speak with me.

"You know that I always try to give a pitcher three complete days of rest between games. Now, Chip has beaten Waseda twice, and he pitched against Hiroshima on Friday. This is Monday, and I guess you could call it three days, even though it is a skimpy three days. Anyway, I've decided to start Chip and hope that he can help us win this one—"

The cheers that interrupted Rockwell's words must have seemed strange to the Waseda players and fans, but it was a spontaneous and indicative response of the team's confidence in their top pitcher.

The game bell clanged again and Waseda left the field, gathering in front of their dugout for the pregame ceremonies. Rockwell waited until the Statesmen quieted and continued, "One more thing: Soapy Smith will do the catching."

CHAPTER 19

A Storybook Finish

SOAPY SMITH was finally behind the plate! The redhead's grin was infectious, and on the mound, Chip didn't even try to hide his smile. Soapy pepped it up, chattering and yelling and kidding with his teammates, unable to restrain his exuberance. Chip tucked his glove under his arm and polished the ball in his bare hands. Then he turned to gaze at the scoreboard. There was a big zero in the top frame of the first inning. Crowell, Minson, and Burke had gone down one-two-three in State's first time at bat.

Chip had faced the Waseda hitters twice previously—in the opening game of the series in Tokyo when he had pitched the no-hitter and again in Yokohama when the Statesmen had whitewashed Waseda 15-0. Today he felt strong and loose.

And, with all of his high school buddies in the lineup for the first time, it was like old times. Soapy was behind the plate, Biggie towered over first base, agile Speed was at shortstop, and Red Schwartz dominated right field.

NO-HITTER

The Waseda players had never seen Soapy catch, and his activity behind the plate—the constant chatter, pep, and wisecracks—kept them off balance. Further, the redhead worked Chip beautifully, keeping the ball low and inside and around the wrists.

The Waseda leadoff batter struck out, the push-along hitter went out on a ground ball from Speed to Biggie, and the third batter lifted a high fly to Fireball. Three up and three down. The score at the end of the first inning: State 0, Waseda 0.

In the top of the second inning, Biggie hit the first pitch, sending a screaming liner straight toward the center-field fence. It looked good for extra bases, but the Waseda center fielder made a sensational running catch and pulled it in for the first out.

Fireball Finley hit one a mile high behind first base, but the Waseda second baseman parked under it and made the catch. Red Schwartz went down swinging for the third out.

The Waseda cleanup hitter led off in the bottom of the second inning. The powerful hitter met Chip's first pitch right on the nose, slamming a line drive over Ozzie Crowell's head for the first Waseda hit of the game. Fireball fielded the ball, and his throw to Crowell held the hitter on first base.

The next batter watched a sharp outside curve go by for ball one. Chip's next pitch was a slow curveball, and the batter met it with a full swing. The ball took off on a line over third base as the runner on first churned toward second. Minnie Minson, playing deep in his third-base position, dove for the ball and made a miraculous backhand catch. Pivoting back, he burned a clothesline peg to Biggie on first base for the double play.

It was a marvelous catch and throw! Minson's brilliant double play made it two away. The next batter lifted a long, high fly to right field. Red Schwartz easily gathered it in for the third out, and State trotted off the field.

Speed Morris led off for State in the top of the third and singled over the shortstop. That brought up Soapy. The redhead took a ball, looked at a strike, and then drove a sizzler over third base for a clean hit. Speed held up on second, and Chip was up with no one down.

Chip walked up to the first-base side of the plate and waited for Coach Rockwell's sign before he stepped into the batter's box. Rockwell had called for a batter's choice advance play, and Chip got ready to bunt. He looked at a fastball around his shoulders for a called strike, took an outside curveball for ball one, and then waited out another high one just above the shoulders for ball two. It was clear now that the Waseda pitcher wasn't going to give him anything good. The next pitch was outside for the three-and-one count, and the umpire waved Chip down to first base when the final throw was too high.

The Waseda infield moved in on the grass as Ozzie Crowell came up with no one down and the bases loaded. Ozzie looked at a low curve for ball one. The next pitch was in there! Ozzie met it with the meat of his bat, sending a hard ground ball straight to the third baseman. The State runners were off with the crack of the bat, but it was a perfect double-play ball.

The hot-corner infielder fielded the ball on the first hop and fired a strike back to the plate to beat Speed for out number one. Then the receiver burned the ball to the Waseda shortstop covering third, and Soapy was out by a stride. Chip held up at second, and Ozzie perched on first. Minnie Minson was now at bat with two away.

Minson was a hard hitter and hard to get out. He had struck out in the first inning and that was his usual quota for a game. He looked at a strike, a ball, another ball, and then singled to right field. Chip was away with the crack of the bat and kept right on going when Rockwell windmilled him around third base. The State dugout erupted with the hit, and when Chip heard their cries and pleas to "hit the dirt" he knew it was going to be close. Ten feet from the plate he took off feetfirst and slid under the catcher just before the ball plunked into the receiver's glove.

"Safe!"

Crowell had moved around to third, and Minson had continued on to second on the throw to the plate. Belter Burke came to the plate ready to help his team. Burke had struck out in the first inning. This time he got hold of a fastball but lined it straight into the glove of the left fielder for the third out.

Chip felt a lot better when he walked out to the rubber in the bottom of the third inning. He had a run behind him, and he knew he could count on perfect support. The comforting, peppy chirping of his teammates came whirling in around him as he took his warm-up throws. When he finished, he walked behind the mound and waited for Soapy's sign.

The weak end of the stick was up for Waseda, and Chip struck out the seventh hitter with three straight pitches. The catcher drove a sizzling ground ball to the left of second base, and Speed made a spectacular glove-hand stop. His throw to Biggie beat the batter by fifteen feet. The Waseda pitcher fouled a fastball back toward the grandstand, and Soapy gathered it in for the third out. The score: State 1, Waseda 0.

State's batters pounded the ball in the fourth inning and every inning after that. But somehow fate seemed to guide every poke directly into the hands of an eager Waseda fielder for an easy out. And when Waseda was at bat, Chip got equally flawless, sensational support.

So the game went into the top of the ninth with State still leading by a single run. Minson led off with a single. Burke drove a high fly to left, but the Waseda fielder pulled it in for the out, holding Minson at first. Biggie looked at a called strike and a ball. On the next pitch, he pulled a screaming grounder across the first-base bag. It rolled out along the right-field foul line for a double. Minson was now on third.

That put runners on second and third with one down, Fireball at bat, and Red Schwartz on deck.

Chip, Soapy, and the rest of the Statesmen lined the apron of the dugout now, cheering and yelling. This was the time to get some run insurance!

But it wasn't to be. Batting lefty, Fireball smashed a low, hard-hit ball toward right field. It looked like a sure hit, but the Waseda first baseman made a one-hand stab, caught the ball, whirled, and threw to second. Biggie was caught off second base for the third out. The rally died before it really began as State took the field for the bottom of the ninth, ahead by the slim margin of Chip's third-inning run.

Chip walked slowly out to the mound and took his warm-up throws. When he finished, Biggie and Speed and Minson and Crowell gathered around, pepping him up, letting him know they were behind him. Out in right field he could hear Red Schwartz yelling his support. He was surrounded by teammates, but the pitcher is always alone out there in the middle of the diamond.

Chip was tired and tight. In four straight throws, he walked the first batter, a pinch hitter batting for the Waseda pitcher. The leadoff hitter came up to the plate with one specific assignment: to advance the tying score to second base. He laid down a drag bunt on the third pitch just to Chip's left. Chip came in fast and tried to pick up the ball with his pitching hand. He fumbled it. So, the tying run was on second base and the winning run was on first, with no one down.

Henry Rockwell called time and walked out to the mound. "Take it easy, Chip," he said. "I'm just stalling to give you a little rest."

His eyes flashed toward the bull pen where Dugan was throwing to Al Engle before he eyed Chip appraisingly. "Are you *sure* you're all right?"

"I'm all right, Coach."

Rockwell deliberated a moment, talking half to Chip and half to himself. "It's my fault. I shouldn't have started you today in the first place." He eyed Chip once more. "Dugan might—" he began.

"No, Coach," Chip interrupted. "I got myself into this hole. I'll get myself out of it."

"All right," Rockwell said briskly. "Go to it!" He turned back to the dugout, and the umpire called, "Play ball!"

The Waseda push-along hitter was up now, and the State infielders moved up on the grass. The batter watched one go by and then got set for the bunt. But Chip had a lot of stuff on the ball, and the result was a pop-up in front of the plate that Soapy gobbled up for the out.

"Atta way, Soapy!" Fireball yelled, his booming voice expressing every State player's relief. All of them were thinking, *Two on and one down* . . . .

Chip got ahead of the next batter, one and two. Then he dealt an outside ball shoulder-high, and the hitter punched a drive over Biggie's head for a clean single. Red came in fast, fielded the ball, and ran in with it to make sure the runner was held on third. Now things were really tight. The bases were loaded with only one down!

The cleanup hitter looked at a ball, a called strike, another ball, and then fouled one high over Soapy's head, clear back against the wire netting of the grandstand.

"I've got it!" Soapy cried. "It's all mine!" He tore off his mask and gathered in the ball for the second out.

Now the stage was set for a Waseda storybook finish. The bases were loaded, with two outs, one run behind in the score, and a power hitter at bat. Chip tried to keep his first two pitches low and got behind the batter in the count, two and zero. The batter watched a strike go by and then another ball.

Pandemonium rattled the stands as Chip called on his screwball. The ball sped for the outside corner and then hooked in and across the plate. The big hitter hesitated and then went for the pitch. But he was too late, cut over the ball, and fouled it back to the grandstand.

Everybody in the stadium was standing now. The Waseda players were out in front of their dugout, and the bleacher fans had spilled over the railing and were pressing out to the edge of the playing field.

Chip breathed a little prayer and backed off the mound. This was it! He got Soapy's sign and toed the rubber. Standing motionless, he checked the dancing runners for a second and then fired his screwball again. The ball went spinning toward the outside corner of the plate, belt high.

Crack! The hitter tagged the pitch with all his power. The ball took off high over Crowell's head and zoomed straight for the right-field fence. Chip took one frantic look and saw Red Schwartz streaking back toward the fence.

"It's over," Chip breathed. "It's a home run."

But he was wrong.

Schwartz and the ball arrived at the fence at the same time. Red leaped high in the air and speared the ball right off the boards just as he charged into the fence with a hard, sickening thud. But even as he slid to the ground, Red held onto the ball. He held it in his glove hand high over his head. And he held the ball up there even as he landed in a sitting position on the ground. He held his glove there for everyone to see until the first-base umpire came puffing up.

Then the umpire's right hand shot above his head. The game was over! It was a 1-0 victory for the Statesmen, and the Waseda series was tied up at three games apiece.

As soon as Red hit the fence, Chip and the rest of the Statesmen ran to help him. But Red didn't need help. He was badly shaken, but he scrambled to his feet under his own steam, still holding his glove hand high in the air.

"Hey, you OK, Red?"

"Are you all right, Schwartz?"

"How do you feel?"

"What's the matter with your arm?"

Red looked around the circle of faces and slowly shook his head. Then he looked up at his glove hand. "Is the ball in my glove?" he asked anxiously.

"Sure!"

"Yes!"

"Of course!"

Red sighed and lowered his arm until he could see the ball. "Honest," he said, raising his arm up in the air again, "I didn't know if I'd caught the ball or not! I just held my glove up there and hoped."

That set the guys laughing as they roughed Red up and got him up on Biggie's and Fireball's shoulders. Then they all proudly marched him to the dugout, kidding with Red as the fans cheered the plucky right fielder.

CHAPTER 20

A Moment for Diplomacy

THE STATE UNIVERSITY baseball team arrived back in Hiroshima Tuesday morning and checked in at the New Hiroshima Hotel. Coach Rockwell gave the players the afternoon off with instructions to report back for a team dinner at six o'clock. After lunch, Chip and Soapy showed a taxi driver the addresses Tamio had given them. They visited the Saito and Okada homes to pay their respects and say their good-byes, enjoying once again the kind hospitality of their friends' parents.

When they got back to the hotel, they stopped by Speed and Biggie's room.

"Coach wants to see you, Chip," Biggie called. "He's in his room."

The maid was just bringing in fresh towels, and the door to Coach Rockwell's room was open. Chip smiled at the sight of his coach leaning back in a patio chair, his feet up on the railing of the little balcony as he looked over the city. "Come in, Chip. Have a chair. Some view isn't it?"

"Sure is, Coach. Biggie said you wanted to see me."

"That's right, Chip. One of the local TV sportscasters wants you to be on his show this evening at eight o'clock. Is that all right with you?"

Thinking of Mr. Fujita, Chip nodded emphatically. "It sure is!"

"Well!" Rockwell exclaimed. "*This* is different. What's happened to you? Usually it's like pulling teeth to get you in the public eye."

"Not this time," Chip said. "I'll be ready."

"Good. Take Soapy with you. They're sending a car around for you at seven o'clock."

The Hiroshima sportscaster had a good studio audience that night. He was enthusiastic and jumped right in. "Hilton-san, have you pitched a no-hitter before the Waseda game in Tokyo?"

Chip nodded. "Yes, sir, in high school."

"You have a fine pitching record in Japan, Hilton-san. You have won five games. You have given your opponents only fourteen hits and allowed only four runs. It is a *fine* record! What do you think of Japan's young college pitchers?"

Standing behind the interviewer, out of sight of the audience, Soapy suddenly began to wave his arms, and Chip nodded imperceptibly. It was exactly the opening he had been hoping for, and he wasn't going to let it get away.

"Waseda and Keio both have fine pitchers," Chip said quickly. "However, I think the best college pitcher in Japan has never even pitched against us."

The sportscaster was visibly surprised. "Who is this fine pitcher?"

"He is from Hiroshima," Chip said. "His name is Tamio Saito, and he is on the Keio University baseball team."

"Why has he not pitched for Keio University?"

"I don't know, sir. He has been pitching for the Keio batting practice, but I have watched him and he's great."

"Young Saito-san is perhaps an apprentice," the sportscaster observed.

"He's in the same class I am," Chip said. "We have both just finished our second year of university studies. Oh, yes! I nearly forgot the most important part. Tamio's senpai also lives in Hiroshima. His name is Yoshiro Fujita, and he was a star first baseman for Keio. He's responsible for Tamio's great ability as a pitcher."

"You know Yoshiro Fujita?"

"Yes, sir. I was fortunate enough to have been a guest in his home." Chip paused briefly. Then, taking a leaf from Soapy's diplomacy book, he continued quickly, "I'll bet if Mr. Fujita was managing the Keio team, he would use Tamio as a starting pitcher. Mr. Fujita sure knows baseball."

"Which of the teams do you think is superior? Waseda or Keio?"

Chip thought furiously. *This is a moment for diplomacy if there ever was one!* Then he made his decision. He had committed himself to Tamio's cause, and he wasn't going to give an inch.

"Keio," he said firmly, "that is, if Keio adds Tamio Saito to its string of starting pitchers."

The interviewer studied Chip speculatively and, after a few more questions, ended the interview. At the end of the program, Chip introduced Soapy to the sportscaster. Afterward, a car returned them to their hotel.

The players took it easy the rest of the evening, sticking pretty close to the hotel. Some of them read, others watched TV, and still others headed for the hotel's business center to check their E-mail. Soapy and Chip had just decided to flip off the TV and get some sleep when someone pounded on their door. It was Coach Rockwell. Down the hall, Greg Garl and Tim Fox were knocking on other doors, and the State players were beginning to congregate in the hallway. Coach Rockwell had decided to treat the team to ice cream, and the players quickly struggled into jackets and tugged sweaters over their heads as they headed down the hall for the elevators.

The next morning after breakfast, Chip and Soapy got ready for their campaign with Mr. Fujita. Chip called his residence, but the maid said he had left early that morning for Tokyo.

"I wonder what that means?" Soapy asked.

"It could mean a lot of things," Chip replied thoughtfully.

Soapy was excited. "Wow! It might mean he went to see the Keio manager about Tamio! Man oh man oh man!"

"And it could mean trouble," Chip frowned. "It *could* mean Tamio will be dropped from the team."

"Why? Because we helped him with his pitching? Chip, I sure hope *we* haven't gotten him into trouble."

"We haven't done anything wrong, Soapy. The whole idea was his. Well, we'll know tomorrow afternoon when we play Keio."

Soapy's face brightened. "That's right," he said hopefully. "Maybe Mr. F went up to see the game."

That afternoon Henry Rockwell started Repeat Phillips on the mound, Patty Patterson behind the plate, Hunter "Spikes" Thompson at third base, and Hans "Dutch" Carter in center field. And he kept the four newcomers in the game the full nine innings. The quartet had played for the freshman team the past spring, and Rockwell had considered them promising enough to bring on the trip.

Phillips pitched a good game, and his freshman team buddies played well, but Hiroshima University got a little better pitching and hitting and won the game, 5-4. It was State's sixth loss in thirteen games.

The Statesmen took the train to Tokyo after dinner. It was the last leg of the trip before they would head for home on Saturday, and anticipation and excitement gripped them. They were a cinch for a spot in the play-off series. Chip's victory over Waseda in Fukuoka had evened that series at three all and assured them of a place.

A victory over Keio Thursday afternoon in Jingu Stadium would eliminate Tamio's team, and State and

Waseda would play for the championship. On the other hand, a Keio victory over State would even their series. In that event, all three teams would be eligible for the play-off games and a sudden-death series would decide the championship. A lot of baseball would cram the next three days for the Statesmen.

When the train pulled into the Tokyo station, Soapy was peering out the window. "Hey, it's Tamio!" he blurted. He turned back and elbowed Chip. "I saw him. He's waiting for us!"

As soon as Chip and Soapy stepped onto the platform, Tamio was beside them. "I will walk with you to the State bus."

As the three friends shouldered their way through the jammed station to the parking lot, Chip and Soapy told Tamio that Mr. Fujita was in Tokyo.

Tamio's eyes widened. "I have not seen him," he said.

"We thought he might have come up to see the game," Chip offered.

"It is always possible," Tamio said slowly, licking his lips. "It could be Fujita-san will talk to the Keio manager." His lips tightened. "Maybe I am off the team."

"Maybe Mr. F will tell him about your pitching," Soapy said hopefully.

"No, it will never happen," Tamio said sadly.

"You never can tell, Tamio-san!" Soapy encouraged.

Keio was just finishing up with their batting practice when State emerged from the player tunnel and headed for the visiting team dugout. Tamio glanced at Chip and Soapy and flashed an OK sign with his throwing hand. Then he turned and walked slowly out to the Keio bull pen.

"Well," Soapy breathed, "so far so good. At least he's still on the team."

"Right!" Chip expelled a mouthful of air in relief.

They waited in front of their dugout while Coach Rockwell called out the batting order. "We'll hit this way:

Crowell, Minson, Burke, Cohen, Finley, Gillen, Morris, Engle, and Dugan—

"Hilton, Dean, and Phillips, throw in the bull pen. Smith and Patterson! Keep 'em throwing."

In a few minutes the game was underway with State batting first. Keio started their number-one pitcher, and he and Dugan waged a pitchers' duel for six innings. Both pitchers received perfect support. Neither team scored. But in the top of the seventh inning, Dugan walked and Ozzie Crowell sacrificed him to second. Minson doubled and Dugan rounded third and sped for home. The throw was close, but Dugan scored.

Then Burke singled and Minson was held at third. The Keio pitcher gave Biggie an intentional walk, and Fireball Finley came to bat with the bases filled. Keio's number-one hurler was clearly nervous, and Fireball drew a walk. That scored Minson for run number two with one down and the bases still loaded.

The Keio manager called time and consulted with the Keio pitcher and catcher. After a few moments, he turned and waved to the Keio bull pen, and his number-two pitcher walked to the mound.

After the number-two hurler took his warm-up throws, Gillen stepped into the batter's box. It was a good spot for the burly right fielder, and Murph tried hard. He looked at a ball and then met a fastball dead center. The pop of the ball in the first baseman's glove followed the crack of the bat so closely it was almost one sound. Finley had taken a good lead, and the double play was automatic. The player on first held the ball and stepped on the bag for the double play. The rally was over, but State was out in front by a two-run margin.

But the lead melted away in the same inning. Dugan's scoring run from second had evidently taken more out of the little pitcher than he could spare. At any rate, he walked the first two Keio batters. It was obvious that Keio would bunt. It was crucial to advance the runners to second and third.

Although Engle worked the batter right, the Keio player laid down a perfect bunt just to the left of the pitcher's mound. Dugan came in fast, fielded the ball, and threw it over Biggie's head. The runner on second scored, but his teammates were held on third and second. The fans went wild!

Rockwell came out of the dugout just as Dugan threw the next ball, but he was too late. The pitch was across the middle of the plate, and the left-handed hitter caught it just right, pulling it up and out over Gillen's head, and over the fence for a home run. Keio now had scored four runs, and there was no one down. The stands were in an uproar.

Coach Rockwell's call for time had come too late. He waved for Dean and waited with Dugan behind the mound. Dean warmed up, and Rockwell and the little pitcher walked back to the dugout.

But Diz was wild. He walked the first batter and hit the second. With the count at three and nothing on the next hitter, the bull pen phone rang again. This time when the redhead hung up, he was all smiles. "He says to hurry up, Chip. He wants us both."

Just then—just as Rockwell shot up out of the dugout— Diz Dean stretched and fired the ball over Engle's head. Al chased the ball, but before he could get it back to the plate, the man on second had scored, and there were runners on third and second.

Rockwell had his time out now, and Chip and Soapy checked the signs as they walked in from the bull pen. While Al Engle took Chip's throws, Soapy put on his catching gear. And when the redhead took the glove from Engle and squatted behind the plate, Chip was ready!

The batter hit the first pitch right back to the mound. Chip drove the runner on third base back to the bag before he pegged the ball to Biggie for the out. One away!

Chip needed only three pitches to strike out the next hitter. But he put too much on his pitches to the next batter and walked him, filling the bases.

"No stress, Chipper," Soapy cried, walking partway up the alley. He held up his index and little fingers. "Two away, guys! Any base!"

Soapy called that one perfectly. The next batter drilled a hard ground ball to Crowell, and the small but compact keystone hustler beat the runner to the bag for the force play and the third out. The score at the bottom of the hectic inning: Keio 5, State 2.

"All right," Rockwell bellowed as the Statesmen trotted in, "let's get 'em back! You're up, Speed," he yelled as he headed for the third-base coaching box. "Make him pitch!"

Speed worked the pitcher for a walk and grinned over his shoulder at Coach Rockwell as he trotted to first base. Hitting in Engle's spot, Soapy singled to right field as Speed went all the way to third. Chip walked over to the first-base side of the plate and got the sign from the Rock. He looked at a ball, took a waist-high fastball for a strike, and then drove the ball through the hole between first and second as Soapy lit out for the keystone bag. Speed scored and Soapy went on to third. Chip was held at first.

The Keio number-two pitcher then walked Ozzie Crowell to load the bases. The Keio manager yelled, "Time!" After a short talk, the manager glanced at the Keio University bull pen and then walked back to the dugout.

"Play ball!"

Minson was at bat. The husky third baseman was an expert at working a pitcher. And when he crouched down, he cut the strike zone down to the size of a Little League chest protector.

The pitcher checked the runners and fired a curve that missed the corner for ball four. Soapy trotted in to score run number four, Chip took third base, and Crowell moved to second. Minson trotted down to first.

A MOMENT FOR DIPLOMACY

The Keio manager called time and was out on the mound again. He and the number-two pitcher exchanged a few words, and then the manager turned and motioned toward the Keio bull pen.

Chip was standing on the bag talking to Coach Rockwell while the manager held the conference on the mound with Keio's number-two pitcher. Chip cast a casual glance toward the Keio bull pen and saw a familiar figure coming in toward the infield. He started to turn back to Rockwell and then whirled for a second look just as Soapy's exuberant shout rang out above the tumult.

"Chip! It's Tamio! It's Tamio!"

CHAPTER 21

The Rising Pitching Star

"WHAT A SPOT," Chip whispered, shaking his head. He watched Tamio Saito walk reluctantly past second base and up to the small group clustered around the mound. It was the top of the eighth, with Keio leading by a single run, the bases loaded with Statesmen, and no one down. This sure wasn't the time and place to make a pitching debut! Tamio's pitching career was in danger of ending before it had a chance to start.

Tamio took his warm-up throws and then stooped to pick up the resin bag. As he straightened up, he shot a quick glance toward Chip and then stepped behind the mound.

It had been only a glance, but in it Chip recognized grim determination. A true sportsman always wishes his opponent well when they meet on the sports field. But once the game is underway, it's a different matter. Real athletes play every game to the max, with no quarter asked and no quarter given. Tamio would pitch his heart out trying to win for Keio University, and Chip would do the same for State.

The fans quieted as they watched the change of pitchers; the relief pitcher was a stranger to them, and they wanted to see how he would fare in this decisive match-up.

Chip studied the Keio players. A few minutes before, they had been pepping it up, shouting encouragement to their number-two pitcher. Now they were silent and fidgeted with their caps, gripped their gloves, and stooped to pick up small pebbles and then toss them away. They attempted anything that would relieve the tension gripping them.

The voice of the announcer drew everyone's attention: "Saito! Tamio Saito is now pitching for Keio University." Then the plate umpire faced the grandstand and lifted his arms. "Play ball!" he shouted.

The Keio infielders were playing up on the grass. Tamio stretched, paused, and then hooked a sharp-breaking curve. It started straight for Fireball's head, and he stepped back. But ten feet in front of the plate, the ball broke down and across the heart of the platter. "Strike one!"

Tamio's next pitch was high and inside and brushed Fireball back. Chip was concentrating on his own play, but he was aware of every pitch. Tamio was keeping Fireball off balance.

Confidence and perspiration etched Fireball's face as he dug in and waited with his bat poised for the next pitch. Minson and Crowell were dancing away from first and second base, trying to distract Tamio.

Tamio paused at the top of his stretch to check Chip and came in again with his curveball. Fireball started to move back but saw the spin on the ball and pulled his bat through in a full powered swing. But he cut under the ball, and the result was a weak pop-up that flew no more than a third of the distance to the mound. It looked as if it were in there for a freak hit.

Fireball dashed for first, and Crowell and Minson took off. Then, as Tamio dashed forward, they hesitated. Chip was a third of the way home. It didn't seem possible that Tamio could reach the ball. But he certainly was trying. Chip held up, ready to continue on for the score if Tamio failed to field the ball and poised to retreat to third base if the ball were caught. At the last second, Tamio dove forward in a reckless belly slide and speared the ball with his bare hand. It was an unbelievable catch, and the crowd exploded with a delighted roar.

Chip didn't see the rest of it. He was too busy trying to beat the ball to third base. He slid safely into the bag just as another tremendous shout erupted from the stands. He twisted around and saw Fireball and Minson walking dejectedly toward the State dugout. Somehow Tamio had managed to get the ball to first base in time to double up on Minson.

"Two away!"

Biggie Cohen was up. But before the big slugger could get out of the on-deck circle, the Keio manager called time.

Behind Chip, in the coaching box, Rockwell grunted. "He's going to put him on," he said. "They're not going to take any chances."

When time was in, Tamio threw four straight balls, and Biggie trotted down to first. The bases were loaded again.

Tamio pitched beautifully to Gillen, keeping the ball low and inside or low and outside. He caught the corners. Murphy looked at a called strike, a ball, another ball, and then missed a low, wicked curveball by a foot. The next pitch was in the dirt and nearly got away from the catcher. The count was now full, and Gillen got ready for the pitch.

Right then, Tamio took a leaf from Chip's book. He came in with a knuckleball. Gillen was set for a control pitch, the fastball, and his swing was too fast. The result was a high foul that the Keio third baseman pulled in for the third out. Tamio had pulled Keio out of an impossible hole!

As soon as the third baseman caught the ball, Tamio's infield teammates surrounded him. They walked him to the dugout, pounding him on the back and roughing him up every step of the way. The fans couldn't get to him, but they stood up and cheered and applauded until he ducked down into the dugout.

Chip wasted no time with the Keio batters in the bottom of the inning. He struck out the first hitter, forced the next to hit a grounder for an easy out from Crowell to Biggie, and set the third hitter down with three straight fastballs. The score at the end of the eighth: Keio 5, State 4.

The Statesmen came running in for their last at-bats. It was now or never. "Let's go, Morris!" Rockwell bellowed. "On deck, Smith! Hilton, in the hole!"

Chip pulled on his jacket and sat down in the dugout to watch Tamio. The debuting pitcher was something to watch. He struck Speed out, worked the count to two and two on Soapy, and then used a change-up that the redhead fouled behind the plate for an easy out.

Chip was up. He couldn't resist an ironic smile as he walked across to the first-base side of the plate. *"This,"* he breathed, "I never dreamed I would see."

Tamio was all business. He knew Chip's ability as a hitter; he had watched him at every opportunity since the first day he had seen him pitch. He kept everything away from Chip, throwing for the corners and keeping the ball in close or far outside. Chip didn't have a chance to hit the ball; he drew a walk in four straight pitches.

The tying run was on first base now, and the Statesmen implored Crowell to bring Chip home. Ozzie worked the count to three and two and then lashed viciously into a lazy curve. He caught the ball solidly, pulling it over third and along the foul line. A little less power or a little more power would have put the ball out of reach of the fielder. As it was, the Keio player cut across the field at full speed, caught the ball on a dead run, and kept right on going to the player's exit.

It was over.

The State-Keio series was all tied up at three games each. All three teams had qualified for the play-off series!

Tamio was waiting beside the State University bus when the Statesmen appeared. But he wasn't alone. Tamio had made it. He had proven that he belonged on the Keio pitching staff. For the first time in his life, he was surrounded by fans. He finally got away from them and pulled Chip and Soapy aside.

Their friend was all mixed up in his emotions. He was proud and humble and hilariously happy. "I owe everything to you, great friends," he kept repeating, "to Chip-san and Soapy-san."

"Hey! What about Mr. F?" Soapy demanded. "Did you see him?"

"No, I did not see him," Tamio said.

"But how come you got to pitch?" Soapy persisted. "Didn't the manager say anything or talk to you?"

Tamio shrugged his shoulders and spread his hands. "He said nothing. He called the bull pen from the dugout and told the catcher to have me ready. It was a big surprise to the catcher and number-one pitcher, and a bigger shock to me." He paused a moment. "I hope Mr. F. saw the game."

"Well, if he didn't, he'll sure hear about it," Chip said.

"I've got something I want *you* to hear, young man," Soapy said, putting his hand on Tamio's shoulder. "The next time you throw that little ol' dinky change-up ball at me, I'm gonna knock it outta the park."

"There will be no next time," Tamio said sadly. "The number-one and number-two pitchers are all right now for the series. They will tell about the series play-off games on TV tonight, at nine o'clock. We will watch, yes?"

"Sure," Chip said. "Come to our room."

"Right!" Soapy added quickly. "But you'll have to translate."

"I'll be there, Soapy-san," Tamio said, grinning happily. "Like you say—count on it!"

That evening, with Tamio translating, the three friends learned that the championship would be decided by a sudden-death series. "They will make the draw for the games now," Tamio said anxiously.

"Who makes the draw?" Soapy asked.

"Coach Rockwell and the Keio and Waseda managers."

The broadcaster continued to talk as Tamio translated. "Waseda has a bye!" he said excitedly. "State plays Keio tomorrow!"

"Well, whaddaya know," Soapy said, rolling his blue eyes. "Here we go again."

"Yes, that is right," Tamio said. "State or Keio will play Waseda for the championship on Saturday."

After a brief silence, Tamio told Chip and Soapy about the big banquet happening on Saturday night at the Imperial Hotel. "Everyone will be there to honor the great State team. But now we have time to visit together, maybe for the last time. Do you have some place you want to go?"

"I know!" Soapy said eagerly. "Let's go some place where we can get—"

Chip and Tamio glanced at each other and burst into laughter. "Sukiyaki!" they chorused.

Every seat in Jingu Stadium was filled the next afternoon when State took the field as the home team against Keio University. Rockwell called upon Diz Dean to start the game, and Diz breezed through the first inning without trouble.

Chip and Soapy were watching the game from the bull pen and could scarcely believe their eyes when Tamio came out of the Keio dugout and walked to the mound.

"Not again!" Soapy exclaimed. "Not two days in a row!"

"He's been doing it all year," Chip said shortly.

"Throwing for batting practice isn't the same as pitching games!" Soapy retorted.

"Maybe not," Chip said, "but it sure helps."

Soapy was right, of course, but he couldn't have proved it based on Tamio's performance. Although the Statesmen got to him for three hits, he whitewashed them for eight straight innings, apparently getting stronger with every pitch.

Keio scored two runs in the third inning on a walk, a double, and an error. They added another run in the sixth on a double, followed by a single to right field. Surprisingly, Dean had good control and pitched well enough to win any game. He had nine strikeouts to his credit going into the top of the ninth, had walked only one batter, and had allowed a mere four hits. It all added up to just too much Tamio Saito.

In the top of the ninth, Diz was terrific, using only thirteen pitches to strike out the three top men in the Keio batting order. State came in for their last at-bat, behind in the score by three. It was the Statesmen's last chance to win the game and stay in the running for the series championship.

Burke was up, Biggie was on deck, and Fireball was in the hole. Tamio had succeeded in handcuffing Burke all through the game, striking him out the first two times at bat and forcing him to pop up to the third baseman the third time. While Tamio was warming up, Rockwell decided to use a pinch hitter and sent Andre "Stretch" Durley in to lead off.

When Tamio finished his warm-up throws, the umpire raised his arms for silence and the announcer said, "Durley! Andre Durley now hitting for Burke."

Durley stood five-six, weighed 160 pounds, batted righty, and was a good hitter. Rockwell was counting on him to get on. Durley did just that, working Tamio shrewdly and refusing to go for a bad pitch. Tamio walked him. The crowd was cheering for Tamio now in one continuous roar.

Biggie started for the plate, and the Keio manager called for time. He talked to Tamio for a few moments, and when the game was resumed, the little pitcher walked Biggie with four straight throws. That put runners on first and second with no one down.

Coach Rockwell took advantage of the walk to call the bull pen. "Soapy? Send Chip in! We might have to use him as a pinch hitter."

The fans in the bleachers stood and applauded Chip as he walked along the fence on his way to the dugout. "Hilton-san! Hilton-san! Banzai! Banzai!"

Fireball walked up to the first-base side of the plate carrying the tying run. In his three previous trips to the plate, Fireball had struck out, flied out to left field, and grounded weakly to shortstop. Tamio made short work of him this time, striking him out with a curveball, an inside fastball, and a change-up.

Rockwell called time and consulted with Chip. The umpire held up his arms for the substitution. The announcer's voice broke through the noise in the stadium. "Hilton! Chip Hilton now hitting for Gillen. Pinchi hitta!"

It was the second time Chip had faced Tamio in the batter's box. In the previous day's game, Tamio had walked him with four balls. Chip hadn't gotten a look at his stuff. Chip eyed Tamio carefully. *Maybe he'll pitch to me today.* Then he put that thought out of his mind. He never, but never, attempted to outguess a hurler.

He was on his own and felt loose and comfortable. State was behind three to nothing, and Coach Rockwell had given Chip the "hit away" sign.

Tamio stretched and zipped his fastball around Chip's knees for a strike. Chip stepped back out of the box. Now he knew. Tamio was under orders to pitch to him.

Tamio tried for the outside corner and a screwball next, but Chip let it go by for a ball. The count was now one and one.

The next pitch was a soft curve that came right in to him just above the knees. Chip went for it, stepping into the ball and taking a full cut. He met the ball right on the nose, and it took off over third base just inside fair territory and headed for the corner in left field.

Durley turned third as Chip rounded first and Biggie reached second. Chip's powerful legs gathered momentum, and he sprinted for second. The Keio left fielder had the ball now and fired it to the shortstop for the relay. Over in the third-base coaching box, Rockwell's arm was frantically windmilling. Biggie headed for home, and Chip waited for the play, poised for the dash to third if the shortstop threw home.

The shortstop caught the ball and pivoted for the throw to the plate. But Biggie was nearly home. The Keio player faked a throw to second to drive Chip back. Then he trotted in with the ball.

Chip turned and looked at the scoreboard just as a big 2 flashed into the bottom frame of the ninth.

Speed Morris was at bat. Speed seldom struck out and was most dependable in tight situations. Tamio was wary and kept the ball low. But on the third pitch, with the count at two and one, Speed tagged a knee-high curve and the ball took flight, heading for the scoreboard in center field. Chip took a short lead and watched the Keio fielder racing for the ball. It was going to be close.

It was close! But the fielder reached up over his shoulder at the last second and pulled in the ball at a dead run. Chip dashed back to second, jabbed a toe into the bag, and sped toward third. The throw was straight and true but too late. He went into third standing up.

Al Engle marched up to the plate with a chance to win the game, but there were two away and it would be tight. Chip guessed that Rockwell had given a lot of thought to a pinch hitter for the big catcher.

Engle swung on the first pitch, fouling the ball off for a strike. He looked at a ball, another one, a called strike, and another ball. Then he backed out of the box.

The fans were going wild! They had found a new star in Tamio, and he had their complete support; their emotions were at a feverish pitch. With a strikeout Tamio Saito could put Keio in the final game to battle Waseda for the championship.

Engle looked longingly at the right-field fence and stepped back into the box. The Keio catcher flashed the sign, and Tamio nodded and fired the ball. There was a sharp crack as the ball sailed on and on into the air and out toward the right-field fence. Chip kept right on going. It was either a home run or the end of State's championship hopes. He turned to look as he neared the plate just in time to see the right fielder park under the ball and make the catch.

The incredible roar of the crowd pounded in Chip's ears as he continued on and crossed the plate. He turned to go out to congratulate Tamio and was nearly knocked off his feet. Hundreds of fans had made their way out onto the field and converged on the little pitcher. And, as if by magic, hundreds more appeared and were on the way. Chip managed to reach the State dugout and, with his teammates, turned to watch. The field was a solid mass of humanity. All were cheering and acclaiming their new pitching sensation, Tamio Saito, who perched high on the shoulders of the crowd.

CHAPTER 22

Tokyo No-Hitter

SOAPY SMITH sprawled dejectedly in the large chair in the corner of their hotel room, his legs outstretched and overhanging the ottoman and his chin on his chest. "Huh!" he said in disgust. "And *you* had to teach him how to pitch!"

"Sure," Chip agreed amiably, sitting on the corner of his bed. "And I'd do it again. So would you, Soapy. You're not fooling anyone." Chip grinned.

Soapy ignored him and continued to glower. "All because of Frank Okada and his dwarf tree," Soapy growled. "Phooey!"

"I wish Frank could have seen Tamio pitch today," Chip mused. "That would have really been something."

"Yeah," Soapy said sourly. "Really something. By the way, where is the guy? It's nearly nine o'clock."

"Give him time," Chip said patiently.

"That's the trouble," Soapy growled. "We gave him *too* much time."

The phone rang and interrupted their conversation.

Soapy pounced on the phone before Chip even got to his feet. "Hey!" he shrieked, grinning delightedly. "Tamio! How you doing, champ? Come on up! We're waiting for you, buddy."

He hung up the phone and turned to face Chip's amused gray eyes. "Aw, Chip," he said sheepishly.

Tamio had been mauled all over Jingu Stadium. Now, as soon as he entered the room, Soapy took up where the fans had left off.

"Please, Soapy-san!" he protested. "I have been hit too much for one day."

"Not during the game," Chip commented dryly.

"Hey, that's good!" Soapy said, nodding at Chip. "Come on, Tamio. Tell us what happened after the game."

"The fans are very happy," Tamio said. "Also the Keio manager and players."

"How about Mr. F?" Soapy asked.

"I did not see Mr. F."

"Didn't the manager have anything to say about your pitching?" Chip asked.

Tamio nodded. "He said I did very good." He paused and continued modestly, a small smile lifting the corner of his lips. "He said I am now the number-one pitcher."

"He did!" Soapy cried. "How about that!"

"It's about time," Chip added happily.

After a few minutes Soapy turned on the TV, and they listened to the details of the afternoon game. Tamio translated the sportscaster's remarks. Chip noticed that in his translation, Tamio said nothing about himself, although Chip clearly heard the words "Saito" and "Tamio" mentioned a great number of times.

Later, just before he left, Tamio tried to thank Chip and Soapy. But, like most young men, he had great difficulty expressing his feelings. At the end, however, he put a little of what was in his heart into words. "I will pitch the championship game tomorrow."

"You what?" Soapy interrupted incredulously.

"I will pitch against Waseda," Tamio continued modestly. "The manager said I can do it."

"But your arm—" Chip began.

Tamio interrupted him. "It is fine, Chip-san. Today every ball I threw was in imitation of Chip Hilton. Tomorrow I do the same thing, the same imitation of Chip Hilton. Every ball I throw against Waseda will be thanks from my heart to Chip-san and Soapy-san."

Before Chip or Soapy could think of something to say, Tamio had bowed and closed the door softly behind him. The two pals sat there a long time and were thoughtfully silent. Right then, Chip and Soapy couldn't have expressed the feeling in their hearts to save their lives.

The cabin lights flickered twice, and the Fasten Seat Belt sign disappeared. "Here goes," Soapy said, elbowing Chip. "I've gotta get this show on the road." He unfastened his seat belt, climbed over Chip, and sprang into the aisle. "Fellow passengers," he cried with a flourish, "give me your attention please."

He held his package up in the air for all to see. "Now, ladies and gentlemen, it says here in Japanese: 'To the great Soapy Smith.' That's me, of course."

Unwrapping the package, he revealed a flat jewelry box. He cautiously released the catch and gazed rapturously at the contents. "Well, whaddaya know," he cried weakly. His eyes widened, and his mouth dropped open in amazed surprise. "Look! A necklace! A pearl necklace for Mitzi!"

Soapy was staggered. But only for a moment. Recovering quickly, he continued, "Well, well, ol' Soapy, the world traveler, is returning from the Orient with treasure for his honey! Ladies and gentlemen, it sure pays to know the right people. Ahem!" He walked along the aisle showing the necklace to his teammates and to the other amused passengers. He missed no one.

Chip moved over into Soapy's seat beside the window and gazed out reflectively at the fleecy clouds. He would never forget the championship game between Keio and Waseda. The Statesmen had left early for Jingu Stadium, but blocks away from the giant field they had been caught in the greatest traffic jam they had ever seen. They finally got through to their box seats just before the pregame ceremony.

The game had developed early into a pitchers' duel. Keio had managed to score a run in the top of the seventh, but Waseda had not been able to do anything with Tamio's assortment of pitches and his marvelous control. He had a perfect game going into the last half of the ninth.

Then, with two down and a runner on second, Tamio had begun to aim the ball. The result was three straight balls. But after a time-out and a talk with the Keio manager, Tamio had struck out the last Waseda hitter to earn a 1-0 victory and pitch a no-hitter.

It had been bedlam then. The crowd had taken over in a wild, frenzied celebration as Tamio was lifted onto shoulders and carried out through the main gate. Chip and Soapy hadn't seen him again until the banquet that night.

The banquet was another unforgettable page of Chip's memories of the tour. A Keio and Waseda player flanked each State player. But Soapy had managed to reverse the process so that he and Chip flanked Tamio. The banquet had been the most lavish Chip had ever attended. Course after course of delicious foods, gifts for everyone, and speeches by the Japanese minister of sport as well as notable sports figures associated with the Goodwill Tour made the night unforgettable.

Yoshiro Fujita had been one of the speakers. He waved aside the translator and, speaking in English, thanked Coach Rockwell and the Statesmen for their contribution to the advancement of Japan's college and university baseball.

Then he congratulated the players. At the end, he mystified everyone except Chip, Soapy, and Tamio by expressing his personal gratitude to Hilton-san and Smith-san for the inspiration they had been to his kohai, the new Keio University pitching star—Tamio Saito.

That had been a real shocker. Tamio, Chip, and Soapy had gasped in amazement. "He knew all the time!" Chip had whispered to Tamio and Soapy. When Mr. Fujita sat down, the three boys had caught his eye and raised their hands in a salute of appreciation.

Chip and Soapy and the rest of the Statesmen had gone to bed early in the morning, completely exhausted but supremely happy. It had started all over again today when they arrived at the airport. There were hundreds of students on hand with all sorts of going-away presents. Tamio had stayed with Chip and Soapy to the very last. Just before they boarded the plane, he had handed a box to each of them.

Chip now opened his box slowly and thoughtfully. Tamio had given Soapy a necklace for Mitzi, and his own box contained a lovely three-stranded choker of cultured pearls. It was a necklace for his mother.

A little card was fastened to the raised center of the box with a pin. Across the card in Tamio's handwriting was a brief message. *From Tamio to the mother of Chip-san.*

Chip removed the card and found a small opening. Something shiny glittered there. He pulled the top open to find a small gold baseball.

He lifted the gold ball from the box and studied the inscription. Glittering black Japanese ideographs were inscribed on a raised band, etched into the surface. And right below was a finely etched seal. Beneath the seal were several more ideographs.

Chip was trying to figure out the ideographs when he heard a familiar voice. "Hello, Chip. Welcome aboard United Airlines." It was Aya Takuchi. Smiling and bowing, she extended her hand. "Well, Chip, your team really made a hit in Japan, especially the player named Chip Hilton. How did you make out with the language?"

Chip was surprised and glad to see Aya. He gripped the friendly flight attendant's hand and shook it warmly. "Fine, thanks to you," he said. "I had a wonderful time and I made a lot of good friends." He held up the gold baseball. "Here, look at this."

Aya took the ball and inspected it carefully. Then she studied the ideographs on the raised band. "I'll say you did," she said, her eyebrows raised. "You met some of the most important people in Japan. Do you know who this seal represents?"

Chip shook his head. "No, Aya, I don't."

Aya held the gold ball almost reverently in her two hands. "The crown prince," she said. "It's his personal seal! How in the world did you meet him?"

"It's a long story," Chip said, "and a wonderful story. What does the inscription say?"

"It says, 'To a fine sportsman.' And it's signed by the crown prince and a Tamio Saito."

They talked a few minutes longer, and then Aya excused herself. "I've got a little work to do," she said, "but I'll sure be back."

The sleek, magnificent plane soared swiftly through the bright, sunny sky, carrying Chip and his teammates homeward and far away from Asia—the land of the Hermit Kingdom and home of the Rising Sun. Chip's spirits fell. He had traveled halfway around the world and found a true friend only to lose him.

As Aya had implied, Tamio was a member of a distinguished Japanese family. He guessed he didn't have to be told that. Especially since he had been privileged to meet the Saito family and to observe Tamio's self-deprecation, gentleness, courtesy, and humble bearing.

Chip leaned back and closed his eyes, but he wasn't resting. He was thinking that the best way for nations to strengthen mutual harmony and understanding was through a common interest so the people of one country could meet with the people of another country, face to face. Baseball was just one of many mediums that could promote the spirit of sportsmanship and international friendship he had experienced.

Just as in business, Chip reflected, goodwill had to be earned. It was the result of years of effort and service and dependability and cooperative understanding. He had found it difficult to grasp many of the Korean and Japanese customs and traditions at first. But as he became better acquainted with Park Bong Kwon and Tamio, the strangeness began to disappear and he could understand them, relate to them. A person couldn't use his own standards to judge those of another country. He had to develop a background and a knowledge of that country's culture and philosophies before he attempted to make a comparison.

He thought about Tamio and Park and all the Tamios and Park there must be in other countries. It was too bad all the young people of the world couldn't have a chance to meet and get acquainted. He would always value the time he had spent on this tour. He had made good friends on the trip, but more importantly, he had made strides for goodwill between his country and other nations.

• • •

TROUBLE STARTS at State University's opening football practices when the famed Touchdown Twins are more interested in personal glory than in team play.

Be sure to read *Triple-Threat Trouble,* the next exciting football story in Coach Clair Bee's Chip Hilton Sports series.

Afterword

ATHLETICS HAVE always played a role in my life. Beginning with my first glove at age five to playing on various teams throughout my youth, inventing dice games for football, baseball, and hockey when dice ruled the sports game market, playing with a tennis ball against the side of the house, or one on one in the driveway—if it was sports related, I was into it! Athletics will always have an effect on me as I watch for those heroes and role models who affect the lives of young people everywhere—today, as they always have!

Having a great love for sports, I read mostly sports stories. A good sports novel was hard to put down, and then only if I was headed to the sandlot. Late in the summer between my eighth- and ninth-grade years, I went in search of a new sports book. I came out of the library with a book called *Touchdown Pass*—a marvelous story about a young man, his friends, and their coach. The young man was Chip Hilton. As I continued through the series of books, I found not only a great athlete, but a great example. At first, I wanted to be a part of the Hilton A. C. and play for Valley Falls, but later I just wanted to be Chip Hilton.

High school athletics play an important role in the overall education of our young people. It gives them the opportunity to be a part of the school and the community. It also provides a way for these athletes to give back to the school as they serve as examples for their fellow students.

As an educator, I have tried to use the things Clair Bee wrote about in the Chip Hilton series: sportsmanship, honesty, integrity, making good choices, and service to our fellow beings. Throughout my coaching years I worked with young players (football, basketball, baseball) to not only enhance their skills, but to help them develop into individuals with character, using the same qualities displayed by Chip Hilton.

I continue to see a need with our young people today: the need for heroes, real and fictional, to provide guidance, help establish goals, and give definition to their lives—the need for examples like Chip Hilton and Coach Rockwell.

I never forgot the books and their lessons. I continually looked for them in libraries, bookstores, rummage sales, etc. I wanted my son to be a part of Chip's world too! I could never find them—until now! The sets I collect today are for my grandchildren and the students at my school so they can reap the benefits from knowing Chip, Soapy, Biggie, Speed, the Rock, and all of the Valley Falls and State University friends. There are great lessons to be learned, and Clair Bee has given us a great way to learn them.

PAT CRISP
Principal, Carson Junior High School
Mesa, Arizona

Sport, Character, and Culture

THE CHIP HILTON SPORTS series celebrates a quality of sport experience that is too often lacking in contemporary sports. Chip is motivated by a love of the game that leads to a respect for all of the participants in the game (coaches, teammates, opponents, and officials) and the things that make the game possible (rules and traditions). For readers interested in learning more about how to encourage such values in your own communities and sports programs, we invite you to contact the Center for Sport, Character, and Culture at the University of Notre Dame. E-mail: cscc@nd.edu.

The Center for Sport, Character, and Culture has a twofold mission. First, it seeks to promote sports as a means for developing and expressing all facets of human excellence, especially moral character, and it also seeks to offer a broad assessment of the role of sport in contemporary culture. In keeping with the spirit of the Chip Hilton books, the center is dedicated to fostering a sense of moral community within sports teams and empowering sport participants to experience the joy and pride of striving for excellence with integrity.

Dr. David Light Shields and Dr. Brenda Light Bredemeier

Your Score Card

I have   I expect
read: to read:

——— ———   1. ***Touchdown Pass:*** The first story in the series introduces readers to William "Chip" Hilton and all his friends at Valley Falls High during an exciting football season.

——— ———   2. ***Championship Ball:*** With a broken ankle and an unquenchable spirit, Chip wins the state basketball championship and an even greater victory over himself.

——— ———   3. ***Strike Three!*** In the hour of his team's greatest need, Chip Hilton takes to the mound and puts the Big Reds in line for all-state honors.

——— ———   4. ***Clutch Hitter!*** Chip's summer job at Mansfield Steel Company gives him a chance to play baseball on the famous Steelers team where he uses his head as well as his war club.

——— ———   5. ***A Pass and a Prayer:*** Chip's last football season is a real challenge as conditions for the Big Reds deteriorate. Somehow he must keep them together for their coach.